Certain Rules

By G.L. Snodgrass

Certain Rules

Copyright 2014 Gary Snodgrass
All rights reserved, including the right to reproduce this book, or portions thereof in any form. No part of this publication may be reproduced, stored in or introduced into a retrieval system or transmitted, in any form or by any means. This is a work of fiction. Names and characters are the product of the author's imagination and any resemblance to actual persons, living or dead, is entirely coincidental.

Purple Herb Publishing.

http://glsnodgrass.blogspot.com

Return to your favorite ebook retailer or the blog linked above to discover other works by G.L. Snodgrass. Thank you for your support

## Other stories by G. L. Snodgrass

Worth Saving
Uncertain Rules
Nothing So Quiet
A Demon's Nightmare

Short Stories

Prom Date
The One That Got Away
Dragon's Skin
The First

**To Ms. Caitlin Snodgrass**

**And**

**Ms. Andrea Reiher**

**May your lives be filled with romance and true love**

Certain Rules

## Chapter One

<u>Scott</u>

There are certain unwritten rules in high school. High on the list, close to the top, is one that says. 'Thou shalt not have sex with your best friend's girl'. - A simple rule, understood by all. - Danny Carrs totally ignored it.

Another rule even higher on the list says: 'Thou shalt not beat the crap out of the star quarterback two days before the play-off game.' I sort of ignored that one. I figured it made us even. Needless to say, the jerks at school didn't see it my way.

They thought they were going to get to me with the silent treatment. The ice cold stares and turned backs were nothing. They hadn't grown up with my grandfather. Their weak attempts didn't get to me. What killed me, a bone deep death, was the laughter and snickering behind me wherever I went.

Scott James, The largest guy on campus, star left tackle, destined for the front line of Nebraska University was a cuckold. Couldn't keep a woman satisfied so she had to go somewhere else.

"Steroids man, it kills it." A high pitched freshman voice whispered.

A stupid sophomore girl fresh from P.E. laughed and said. "You know I heard they used him for the model when they made Shrek, only they had to tone it down for the movie, it scared all the kids."

"I hear he's so dumb he didn't know how," was heard repeatedly.

The fact that she hadn't ever let me try made it worse.

I'd caught best bud, Danny Carrs and the love of my life, Miss Gina Woods, in his room the previous afternoon. She had her legs strait up in the air with Danny between them, pumping away like a locomotive going uphill. There are some sights that burn their way into your brain and you'll never get 'em out.

I'd come to Danny's to borrow a chemistry book; the world knew he'd never need it. The boy hadn't cracked a book in the nine years I knew him. He had his head banging music going full bore and never heard me knock. I stepped in, the room smelt like old socks and Ben Gay ointment. Gina screamed, Danny cursed, jumped up, and held out his hands as if to say, 'it's not what you think man'.

Unfortunately it was exactly what I thought man, I saw red and swung.

I've got to give him credit, he didn't stay down. Not a very a smart move. But then Danny wasn't a renowned genius.

He's your typical Greek god. – Brown curly hair and green eyes, six-one, hundred eighty. I'm more your Norse variety with black hair and the beginning of a straggly red beard. I had him by three inches and seventy pounds; All of it pure muscle from a lifetime of slinging hay bales and four years of banging into fellow giants on the gridiron. Danny on the other hand made Justin Beiber look like an ugly slug.

He jumped up and threw a quick jab. His fist hit me square in the jaw and I heard the bones in his hand crack with a sickening snap. The boy had never learned how to throw a punch. I'd been doing his fighting for him since fourth grade, both on and off the football field. But he tried. I smiled and returned the favor with a left to the eye and a right to the ribs. He crumbled like a sack of potatoes dropped from the roof.

And with that the red rage left me to be replaced by a deep burning hurt. How could they do this to me? What did I do? I hadn't felt this kind of gut wrenching loss since my parents were killed seven years earlier.

Gina knelt on the bed in all her naked glory, hiding behind a too small pillow. This was not how I anticipated seeing her naked for the first time. Long black hair messed up in the ultimate bed head and white porcelain skin that looked purer than a fresh January snow.

Her head swiveled back and forth between Danny and me as if watching a tennis match. Her mouth open in shock and her eyes clouded in confusion. Slowly awareness started to return and her eyes turned to fire. She screamed and jumped off the bed to cradle Danny's head in her lap. "What have you done you giant oaf?" she yelled as if everything was my fault. She forgot about me and returned to brushing the hair from his eyes.

I so wanted to come back with a witty retort, a small pithy saying that would put her in her place. Something that would go down in history as the smartest thing a guy in my situation ever said. If not that, at least something to take away the pain. Or better, something to hurt her as much as she'd hurt me.

I had nothing. Nada. I stood there, my knuckles screaming, gob smacked with realty. No nothing. I never had anything when it came to talking to girls. Maybe this is why I ended up in situations like this.

My fists clenched, I hated her so much. She'd ruined everything.

I felt like a worthless piece of crap. The red rage started to return. One of the few things I'm proud of that night is the fact that I somehow got myself under control. Letting out a big sigh I turned and stomped out.

It had become hard to see, everything had gotten all misty. I made my way out of there and to my truck and home to the farm. My sister Mattie looked up as I stormed in, yelling that I wasn't hungry. It probably raised a few red flags. I hadn't missed a meal since I'd had my tonsils out at age three. They gave me space. They could see something was wrong and left me alone. Grandfather even did my chores for me without giving me a ration of crap about it. He'd get me later I was sure.

The next morning at school was interesting to say the least. The hallway full of students parted like the red sea before Moses. That sweet aroma of floor wax and teenage hormones washed over me as I walked down the canyon feeling every pointed barb and hateful glare.

Of course everyone knew what happened, or at least some twisted version. To them I had become the monster who ruined their chance at shared glory. Taken any chance of a state championship out of the realm of possibility. The beast of the night, too big and too dumb to know what I'd done.

They didn't realize the half of it and just how close I came to losing it. I could feel the anger building in me like a raging forest fire. My heart raced, and my muscles were tighter than a drum. I wanted to hit something, hard. Desperately needed to crush something. Anything to make this pain go away.

I'd thought she cared. She'd been my first steady girlfriend. She'd approached me first for Christ's sake. Coming up to me at last summer's quarry party. Acting like I was something important. Staring at me through those long lashes, making feel like I was special. It'd all been a scam to get close to Danny. I could see it now. She'd always wanted to know what he was up to, who he was seeing.

It was Gina that announced our couple hood on Facebook after two dates to the movies. She was the one who said I love you first. It was her that said she was saving her virginity until marriage. A fact that I could reluctantly accept. I'd have done anything to make her happy. People treated me differently because of her. If Gina Woods was my girlfriend I must be pretty special, almost normal.

And my best friend Danny, the bastard. We'd gone to war together on the field. I protected his back and he shared his fame and glory. What had I done to them? Where did I screw up?

I found myself sitting in Mrs. Hollis AP History class wondering how the hell I got there. A quick glance at the clock said we only had a couple of minutes left. Earth to Scott, get your shit together boy, it's going to be a long day and you're going to need to focus.

A short beep over the intercom made everybody jump and look at the speaker on the wall.

"Mrs. Hollis, please send Scott James to my office, thank you," a grumbly voice said. There weren't any laughs, no snickers, not even a whoop whoop. Everybody knew what this was about and were hoping for the worst. A sea of gleeful smiles and hateful eyes watched me leave. Only Katie River seemed to be on my side. Her sorrowful eyes looked like she was watching a puppy being taken to the execution chamber.

One out of twenty five was more than I expected. The rest of them stared and remained silent as I gathered my stuff and headed out the door before the teacher could say a word. It's not like I didn't expect it.

The hallways were as barren as an Arizona desert and my steps echoed off the lockers as I made my way to the Principal, Mr. Turner's office. Would the cops be there? I could see it now. Being led out of the school in cuffs, hands behind my back. Everybody standing there cheering and yelling junk. Screw it, things couldn't get worse.

I glanced into Mr. Turner's office and realized how wrong I could be. Grandfather sat in one of the chairs. My stomach dropped to the floor and I had a hard time swallowing. Crap, this had gotten so much worse. The thought of disappointing him made me break out in hives.

Old battle axe Betty, the principal's secretary and the center around which the school revolved nodded her head that I should go right in. Her eyes narrowed in scorn and I thought for sure I'd melt before I made it to the door. I gave a quick knock and entered.

My grandfather raised an eyebrow as I entered, at least he didn't look like he hated me. Not yet, they mustn't have told him.

"Scott, thank you for coming," the principal said indicating I should take the remaining free chair. A cough behind me startled me for a moment. Coach Carlson followed me into the room, firmly closing the door. He wore his normal coach cloths, white polo shirt and red shorts with tube socks and tennis shoes. His friggin whistle hung around his neck. Did he ever take it off? The man probably wore it to bed and used it any time Mrs. Carlson got out of bounds.

I sat next to grandfather. The chair felt hard and unforgiving. The room smelt like paper and maybe a faint hint of tobacco, Mr. Turner had been sneaking cigarettes again. He looked at the coach and then at my grandfather. He seemed to be avoiding looking at me.

"Mr. James, thank you for coming in so quickly," he said.

My grandfather, the official 'Mr. James', nodded his head. He never did go in for the simple pleasantries of conversation.

Taking a deep breath Mr. Tuner brought his hands together. Interlocked his fingers and set them on the desk in front of him. "Yesterday, your grandson, beat a fellow student, Danny Carrs. He hurt him so bad that the boy had to be taken to the hospital. They operated on him this morning and he should be released later this afternoon."

"Two days before the play offs," Coach Carlson snapped from behind us.

My grandfather didn't say anything, just looked at the principal and waited for the rest. I could see his hands griping his jeans. His knuckles were turning white. Boy was he pissed. To show that much emotion said a lot.

"As you can imagine, we can't have our students fighting. Especially young men who should be setting an example. I am afraid I am going to have to Expe..."

"Hold it a second," my grandfather said, shocking me with his gravelly voice. He didn't normally interrupt people.

"Yes Mr. James?" the principal asked, his eyebrow rising.

Grandfather stared at the principal for a moment his eyebrows furrowed in concentration. "Did this fight occur on school grounds?"

"It wasn't a fight, it was a beating. Our most important player no less. Scott's supposed to be protecting him, not putting him in the hospital," Coach Carlson said.

My grandfather turned in his chair as his eyes narrowed and his brow creased. He shot the Coach a look that could freeze water on a warm day. "I remember you getting into a fight or two in your younger days, Jake. In fact, if I remember correctly, Scott's dad kicked your butt in 8th grade after he caught you bullying some of the smaller boys."

Coach Carlson sputtered for a moment. I hadn't known that about dad and Coach. That might explain a couple of things.

"That was kid's stuff, this is way more serious," Coach said.

"Why, because of who got hurt, or the fact it happened a couple of days before a football game?" Wow, I couldn't believe this, the old man stuck up for me. Of course that was all going to change when he found out why.

Grandfather had always told me that a man who couldn't control his emotions wasn't much of a man. That I was responsible for what I did. No excuse. He'd also drilled into me the fact that a guy my size had a special responsibility of staying in control. People could get hurt otherwise. Danny most definitely proved that last point.

Grandfather turned back to Mr. Turner. He hadn't asked what the fight was about. Hadn't looked at me to see if I was all right. He'd just assumed what the principle said was true.

"And why aren't the police here?" Grandfather asked, pausing for a moment. "I assume Danny's dad decided not to press charges. That must mean his old man's embarrassed about something. Either the fact that his precious son got his ass kicked. Or the reason behind the fight. Probably both."

Mr. Turner sighed. "We don't know the reason. Maybe Scott would like to enlighten us?" They all looked at me as if I had the answer to the meaning of life and was holding out on them. I stared back but didn't say a word. They would learn soon enough It surprised me they hadn't heard the story already.

Turner's eyes glinted and I realized the bastard had heard. He wanted me to say it out loud. My virgin girlfriend preferred to have sex with my best friend instead of me. I'd always thought he was a bit of an asshole. It wasn't until that moment that I knew how much.

I took a deep breath and got ready to let loose on them. To tell them what I thought about their friggin school and where they could put it. They didn't care about Danny or me. It was the fact that we might have brought the school and therefore the town a trophy. Some brass statue to be put in the front case where Mr. Alverez, the janitor would dust it off twice a year. I could feel the rage rising like a coke bottle ready to explode.

A bony hand grasped my arm. My Grandfather's gnarled fingers held me back. It shocked me, how old they looked. Brown age spots had appeared on the back of his hand. When did that happen? I'd seen those hands twist barb wire into shape one day then sooth a struggling heifer as she gave birth the next.

I looked into his eyes and saw a glint of something I didn't understand.

"Actually Mr. Turner. I don't believe you can punish Scott, it didn't happen during school or on school grounds," My grandfather said as he leaned back in his chair.

Turner looked as if someone had let the air out of him and stared at his hands.

"It might not have happened on school grounds. But I can sure do something about it." Coach Carlson said from his perch behind us. "Scott signed a contract at the beginning of the season, all of the boys did and promised not to do anything that hurt the team cohesion. I think this qualifies. Scott is off the team. Period."

My gut clenched into the tightest knot. I figured this would probably be the case. To actually hear the words felt like a helmet to the middle. I stared out the window like it didn't mean a thing. Hell, I'd have taken an expulsion if it meant I could have stayed on the team. They couldn't do anything worse.

"What's more," Coach continued. "I plan on calling Coach Steven's at the university and letting him know what has happened. I'm pretty sure you can kiss that scholarship goodbye."

I swear to god he sounded like a little kid.

Well there it was, the final whistle, game over. I'd been waiting for it ever since I threw that first punch the day before. My one way out, my one dream, gone. Just like that.

I felt a new loss, one more thing piling onto all the losses. This was different. Losing that scholarship was letting my dead parents down. They'd met and gotten married while at the University of Nebraska. Both of them would light up like roman candles whenever they talked about their time there. They'd shoot each other a secret glance and smile at some shared memory.

I wanted to go to Nebraska so bad it hurt. I wanted to start for their football team. I wanted to be what Keith Jackson had famously dubbed "A Big Ugly up front." Hell, secretly I wanted to parlay that into a pro football career. I know I might be stretching it a little, a guy could dream couldn't he? Or at least I could until I threw that first punch.

An empty, hollow dullness descended over me. It felt like a hole had opened inside of me, sucking my soul into a giant chasm. My mind searched for an out, anything. But there wasn't a thing I could do about it.

My grandfather stood and threw Coach Carlson a nasty look. I thought he wanted to say something. He hesitated, then shook his head. "If that's it, we'll be going," he said as he turned and walked out the door. I looked at Turner and Coach before I jumped up to follow the old man out.

Battle Ax Betty looked like she was going to swallow her tongue. I'm sure Turner would fill her in later. I caught up with Grandfather at the front door and followed him out to his truck parked at the front of the building. I didn't know what I was supposed to do now. My thoughts were tumbling around like a clown in a barrel.

"You don't got to tell me, but, I've got to admit I am dying of curiosity," Grandfather said. "I mean, it's not like you and Danny to get into it like this."

He'd caught me flat footed. I hadn't thought this through, or at least not to a way that made any sense. How could I tell him that I had lost control? Especially about something like this. A chill traveled up and down my spine when I thought about saying the words.

The birds were chirping and I could taste potential rain. I realized I was stalling. The old man stood there with his hands behind his back patiently waiting.

I took a deep breath and told him everything. About how I found them. About how Gina had never wanted to do anything more that kiss, and how she hadn't even seemed to like that. When I finished I hung my head and stared at the ground. The deafening silence eating into my soul.

We reached his truck and he suddenly halted before he glanced at the sky. He did that before he made any decisions. I used to think he searched for god's guidance. It took me a few years to realize that he instinctively looked at the weather. No farmer ever made a decision without checking the weather. Our lives revolved around it.

His gnarled hand came into my vision. He stood there waiting for me to shake it. I reached out and grasped it. My heart lodged in my throat when I realized that mine was as big as his. We squeezed and he stared into my eyes. "Your dad would have been proud" was all he said. Not that he was proud, not that he felt my pain.

Hey, I'll take it. One of my most important rules is – Any approval from Grandfather was the equivalent of winning the Heisman and an Oscar on the same day.

## Chapter Two

<u>Katie</u>

Whoever said high school wasn't fair, didn't know the half of it. High school ranks right up there with 'life' in its unfairness. It's one of those rules that no one ever tells you about until it's too late.

The poor idiot, Scott I mean, come on. Anyone could have told him what was going on. Even someone like me on the outside, the extreme outside, could see she was using him to get to heart throb Danny. The way she'd light up, giggling at every lame joke, flirting whenever Scott wasn't around. It was a farce until it became a tragedy. The Greeks would have been proud.

It was ten minutes into first period before I knew what was happening. I sat immediately behind Jennifer Hobson and Marla Jackson. Two of my best sources of Intel. I used my tricks to remain invisible. Letting my hair fall across my face. My eyes focused on the front of the room. As far as they were concerned I didn't exist. Just the way I liked it. I sneaked a handy wipe packet and opened it under my desk before sanitizing my hands while I listened.

"He caught her in bed with Danny," Jennifer said.

"No way, for reals? Wow, I thought she was the holy of holies," Marla questioned.

"Yeah, but it was Danny Carrs, who could blame her." Both girls laughed. "Johnny told me. He visited Danny at the hospital."

"Marla, Jennifer, please pay attention," Mr. Lavers said from the front of the room. I could have kicked him.

Me? I observe. It's safer out here on the fringes. 'Don't get involved' is the rule I live by. It's served me well so far. Better to watch other people crash and burn.

I saw everything from the edge. I could usually tell who was going to break up with whom long before they knew it themselves. Who was on their way out of the in group? I could tell you who cheated on their Spanish test this morning and who worried about taking a pregnancy test this afternoon. The one test you couldn't cheat.

I knew which kids were getting abused and which were higher than a kite. I knew who broke into the lockers during last week's football game and who was going to be next year's valedictorian. I mean, I saw it all and kept it to myself.

Knowledge like that left me feeling a little guilty about not warning him. Scott had always been nice. I mean, it's not like we talked or anything. It's just that he'd never been mean, never gone out of his way to make fun of the strange new girl.

I ran into him once in the hall. Literally ran into him. It was like walking into a brick wall at full speed. Totally my fault, I was looking at Jessie Taylor and her brother fight about something and didn't see the mountain in front of me. My books went flying one way and my glasses the other.

He never commented about my beet red face. Not a word about my stammering apology. He acted like it was all his fault, apologizing as he helped me retrieve my stuff.

Like I said, a nice guy. And you've got to admit that's unusual for a jock.

He sat at the front of the class in fourth period and stared at the front wall. His shoulders straight and head up like he didn't have a care in the world. I could tell though, like I said, I observe. The tips of his ears were cherry red and his fist would clinch and his knuckles turned white every time somebody made a snide comment. I don't know how he made it through the class without exploding. Instead, at the bell he calmly stood up, gathered his books and slowly walked out the door. Everyone jumping to get out of his way. It was strange, as if I was proud of him. Not enough to get involved though.

.oOo.

I've always thought of the library as mine. The one place that was free of the teenage angst and drama that permeated everything around here. There is this smell, it's not strong enough to be called an aroma. It's a simple smell. Paper, glue and leather binding with a faint taste of copy toner. - Come on, you've smelt it. Is there anything calmer, less dramatic than a library? The room enfolds you like a warm blanket that promises to keep the world outside. God I love that place.

So imagine my surprise to find Scott James parked at a center table in my library. He hadn't picked a table in the back. No not him. It has to be right there in the middle of the room. Was the guy a born masochist? My stomach fluttered a little. I didn't need drama in my library. As the TA for the library during sixth period, my job was to eliminate drama. Helping Mrs. Johnson. Mostly returning books to the stacks and helping freshmen find their way around. It was my favorite part of school and Scott James was going to ruin it by sitting in the middle of my library.

He'd hung his red and white Letterman jacket over the back of his chair. He looked up when I came in and our eyes met for a brief second, nothing. No reaction, like I said, I'm very good at being invisible. Turning back to his book, he flipped a page and returned to his own world.

I ducked behind the counter as I ripped a package open and pulled out a handy wipe for my hands before I started processing books, sorting them into categories. I let my hair fall in front of my face so I could peak through it at Scott. It was one of my many tricks at staying hidden.

I'll admit it, I was worried about him. How did someone fall from the top to the bottom without cracking up? You know that whole, "those the gods wish to destroy, they first make mad" thing.

No one would ever call him drop dead gorgeous, but he was good looking, in that rugged, manly sort of way, His thick black hair kissed the tops of his ears. He kept swiping at it like it tickled. He had an old scar below his right eye and a faint bruise on the left side of his face. It seemed that heart throb Danny had gotten in at least one punch before his world became seriously disturbed.

I found myself staring at Scott and forgetting about what I was supposed to be doing. I mean the guy was huge with shoulders wider than the Grand Canyon and hard tanned arms the size of small trees. They weren't those sculpted weightlifter muscles. These could only be built with years of hard work outdoors.

He had soft chocolate eyes that hid a deep intelligence. It always surprised me to see someone so big with an intelligent look. It wasn't normal.

His brow creased in confusion and he went back a few pages to reread something, found what he wanted and nodded to himself. I wondered what he was reading. It didn't appear to be a text book. I had an almost overwhelming urge to go over and ask.

Whoa Katie, what is going on? You do not get involved. Ever. And talking to Scott James was way too much involvement. Suppressing a shudder and fighting to get my rebellious stomach back under control I returned to what I was supposed to be doing.

Mrs. Johnson had gone to a meeting and left me a note asking me to process some new books. I glanced to the two boxes on the floor and sighed in resignation. Why did they ship the books in such big containers? I could never get them up on the desk until I'd half emptied them. I didn't even try to pick one up, instead I started pushing and dragging the first box to the front desk.

"Do you need a hand with that Katie?"

A deep voice from behind me made me jump. After I came down from the ceiling and got back into my own skin, I turned and saw Scott standing there with a questioning tilt of his brow. Okay, two things popped into my mind simultaneously. One, did he know I'd been staring at him, and two, he knew my name! I hadn't thought he knew I existed, let alone my name.

"What?" I answered, demonstrating my outstanding ability with the English language. I wanted to melt into nothingness.

He looked at me with a deep frown and shook his head. "I'm sorry, didn't mean to scare you, I... I just wanted to help. If you need it that is? But hey, I understand." He turned and started back to his chair before I could get my brain back into working order.

"No! …. I mean yes, I could use a hand. Thank you." The words came out without me processing all of the ramifications. I knew I couldn't let him walk away thinking I was afraid of him. The fact that he terrified me, not that I thought he'd ever hurt me, more on that stomach fluttery level that scared the bejesus out of me.

He nodded and stepped behind the front desk. Bent over – I won't say anything about how excellent his jeans looked when he bent over - and placed one box on top of the other. He picked them both up and turned to me.

I, being infinitely cool, just stood there gawking. I could barely move one and he picked up two of them like they were puff cakes. We stared at each other for a moment before I realized he was waiting for me to tell him where to put them. My face flushed red and I pointed to a clear spot on the counter.

He placed the boxes on the desk, dropping one next to the other, dipped a small nod with a charming smirk then turned and walked back to his book. My heart raced a little, Okay a lot. I was pretty sure that it was going to beat right out of my chest and fall on the floor at his feet. That silly smirk that said, 'what you going to do, life sucks, then you die.' Obviously, the boy got it.

We spent the rest of the period ignoring each other. I'd sneak a peek, hoping to catch him looking at me. But every time he had his head buried in his damn book. I noticed that he used a book mark and didn't dog ear the page. Another major plus in his favor. It wasn't until the bell rang and his sister came in that I realized I'd never thanked him for helping move the boxes. How much of an un-cool idiot could I be? He probably thought I was a self-centered airhead. Or worse, that I despised him and was just using his muscles to my benefit.

His younger sister was a freshman with long brown hair and a peaches and cream complexion. I didn't know much about her other than she rode to and from school with her brother. Her eyes creased when she first stepped into my library. I could tell she was worried about him but she didn't say a word as she waited for him at the door.

He gathered his book and joined her then turned towards me and caught me staring. He gave me another nod and that death defying smirk. They both left my library and a quietness settled into the room.

I watched them go and my mind drifted. To what could have been, to what my life should have been like.

Shaking my head to clear it of cobwebs, I placed a new book into my backpack and zipped it shut. Once I had it closed it all the way, I immediately opened it and closed it again. Three times I did this before I could leave. Sometimes it sucks being me.

## Chapter Three
<u>Scott</u>

I'm a big believer in setting goals. Do more lifts today than yesterday. Straight A's, that type of thing. Well now I had a new goal. Make it through this last year of high school without killing anyone.

The cafeteria had become my own personal crucible. I made a point of ignoring them. All my former friends. The guys who had my back. The girls who used to smile at me, ask me my opinion about their loves lives. I ignored their nasty looks and whispered comments.

Even the cafeteria lady in her hair net and stained smock gave me the stink eye when she plopped a spoon of mash potatoes onto my tray. She used to give me an extra-large serving. This time they looked like a marshmallow's worth. Plus she forgot the gravy. Did you ever try to eat cafeteria mashed potatoes without gravy? It ranks right up there with wall paper paste.

Loading my tray with a couple of sandwiches, two bags of chips and a piece of apple pie. I paid another upset lunch lady and ambled into the main room as if I didn't have a care in the world. No way I'd let them think they were getting to me. You'd have thought that after five days they'd get tired of this crap. But no, the silent stares and sickening snickers continued.

I chose a middle table in the dead center of the room. Within seconds kids were cramming food down their throats so they could get out of there. It was like I had the plague or something.

One of the departing girls left a whiff of sickening sweet perfume. What was it about girls, they covered themselves in some sugary bubble-gum scent and thought it made them sexy. That was one of the things I liked about Gina. She wore a rose lavender mix, always just the right amount. It was sexy as hell and used to drive me up the wall. I closed my eyes for a moment and floated back to that soft smell.

Get a grip Scott, you're in the middle of the cafeteria for Christ sake. I remembered the smell of roses and lilacs in Danny's room and my heart hardened a little. Hell it was as hard as a rock. I absently ate my lunch while staring them down, daring them to say or do something.

"You know if the wind changes, your face will get stuck that way," Katie the library girl said as she sat at my table and opened a brown paper lunch bag. Obviously referring to my permanent frown.

"Um, you know its social suicide sitting there right?" I asked, glancing around to try and figure out what was going on. The girl hadn't said two words to me for two years, and she sits down like she owns the place.

She chuckled and flashed the hint of a pretty smile. "Oh I've been dead to them for years."

"No, I'm serious, this is not smart."

She smiled again and finished emptying her bag one item at a time. First half a sandwich that looked heavy on the lettuce, a yogurt and a plastic spoon, and finally a green apple.

"Listen Katie, you should probably move to another table." She totally ignored me. "Hey, since when do you eat in here anyway?" I asked and glanced at the popular table, maybe they hadn't noticed.

Of course they all had their heads together discussing the library girl and the traitor.

Katie glanced over her shoulder to see what I was looking at. "They're planning on jumping you," she said like they were making a trip to the Kmart in the next town.

I winced, her comments were not surprising but they still hurt. "Hmm, let me guess, John, Jason, and Tommy?" I said.

"Yes, how'd you know?"

"Simple really, John's the only one with the balls to even think about trying. Jason's dumb enough to go along, and Tommy will act tough but stand on the sidelines and egg them on. You've got first period with John's girlfriend Nicole. She was probably bragging to Jenny Pearson.

"Wow impressive. You don't seem too worried."

I shrugged my shoulders. What could I do? We continued to eat in silence. I'd lost my appetite, which happened a lot lately. John had been a good friend. We'd played next to each other on the offensive line. Gone fishing together last summer a couple of times. I hated the idea of getting into a fight with him, It wasn't right.

I looked at the girl across from me, really looked. She was pretty, but I already knew that. I noticed the big green eyes and the high cheek bones. Here hair was long, a pretty reddish brown color. I think they call it auburn with a bit of a natural curl. She had a habit of pushing it out of her eyes and behind her ear but it would be back in front a few seconds later.

"Why are you telling me this stuff? Believe me, I'd have figured it out soon enough.

Now she shrugged her shoulders. Her cheeks turned a little pink as she focused on her food in front of her.

"I feel a little guilty," she said.

"Why?"

She hesitated for a moment. I could tell she was embarrassed. "Because I didn't tell you about Gina."

"You couldn't have known."

She looked at me like I was a patient escaped from an asylum. "Everybody knew, correction, anyone who knew anything about her and paid any attention."

Great, not only was I with a cheating bitch. Now I learned that everyone had been laughing at me for months. I threw my spoon and the last half of the last sandwich onto my tray. I was getting so tired of all this crap. How is it that a guy could get all the way to eighteen years of age and be so dumb? I shook my head and tried to ignore them all.

Before I could run away in my mind. My little sister had to sit down and ruin it all.

"What are you doing here? We talked about this, remember," I said to her. The last thing I needed was Mattie's life being ruined because of me. I glanced at Katie to see if she might support me on this. She looked at her lunch acting as if she wasn't there.

Mattie flipped her brown hair behind her shoulder and finished sitting down. Her brow creased in a frown as she shook her head. "If she gets to sit here, then I get to."

My sister always was relentless. She'd been on me for days to let her sit here with me during lunch so she could show the school that at least one person supported me. I loved her more than anything, but there was no way she got involved in all this.

Ever since our parents had been killed in a car accident we'd been closer than most siblings. Living with Grandfather drove us together. I know she worried about me. She'd never really liked Gina. I'd chalked that up to her having a school girl crush on Danny. She'd always worshiped the ground he walked on. However, even my fifteen year old sister was smarter than me when it came to Gina.

"Hi, I'm Mattie," she said, holding out her hand for Katie. "Seeing as how my big brother has the manners of a brick, I thought I should introduce myself. You do know its social suicide to sit her, right? Hey, you're the girl from the library aren't you?"

Katie's eyes grew to the size of beer coasters at the exuberant young girl who had sat next to her. She reached to shake her hand and said, "Hi I'm Katie."

"So why is she sitting here?" Mattie asked me. I knew she was trying to change the subject and hoped I'd forget she'd placed herself here in the middle of the battle zone.

"I'm here to warn you brother that the cool kids are planning on jumping him later." Katie said.

"Jesus, she doesn't need to hear about all this," I said. "It doesn't matter anyway, they're not going to do anything for a while. They'll wait until Danny comes back."

"How do you know? You can't be sure. You should tell someone. Come on Scott, this is serious." Mattie said. Her face scrunched up in that worried look she got whenever something bothered her.

"She's right," Katie added while opening her yogurt.

"She doesn't need your help Katie. Neither of us need your help." I said with a little too much anger. I wasn't mad at them. I was pissed off that they were involved in a bad situation. A strong protective urge came over me whenever I thought of either of these two young women being hassled or disturbed. I could understand the feeling about Mattie, it was sort of surprising though to be feeling it for Katie Rivers.

Katie blanched and her face turned white at my harsh words. Before I could apologize we were interrupted again.

"Hey Mattie, mind if I join you." A pimply faced ginger haired boy slid into the seat next to Mattie before she could answer. He adjusted his tray and smiled at me. "So what's everybody talking about?" He asked like we were discussing the chance of rain. The boy either had the brains of a goat or the balls of a bull to be sitting here now.

Mattie's face turned beet red and her lips were locked in a tight line. This was a first, a speechless Mattie was not something you saw every day.

"Hi, I'm Kevin Hays," he said. "You know my older brother, Jason. He's the dumb idiot over there," he said nodding toward the popular kid table. The boy was all elbows and freckles with a long lanky frame and bright eyes that didn't miss a thing.

You could have knocked me over with a warm breeze. "Do you have any idea what you're getting yourself into?"

"What?" He answered with a mock sense of innocence. "The edict from on high that no one is allowed to talk to you or face the wrath of those that matter?" He shrugged his shoulders as if it didn't concern him.

"Yes that," I said as I looked at Katie to catch her staring at me, her eyes twinkling while she suppressed a laugh. It made me want to laugh too.

"Well I figured this would be my chance to sit next to Mattie," he said. "You can't blame me now can you? I mean, come on. Think about what this is going to do for my reputation in the freshman class. I ignore the edict from on high, confront the big bad brother, and most of all, I actually get to sit next to the goddess who is Madison James," He said before stuffing half a sandwich into his mouth.

Definitely balls like a bull I thought.

Katie snorted and brought her hand to her mouth. Mattie looked like she wanted to melt into the floor. I caught her sneaking a glance at him from beneath her brow and a flash of appraising interest. Oh Christ, my kid sister was interested in a boy. And worse, a boy was very interested in her. The protective emotions kicked into high gear. My hands clinched into fists without me thinking about it.

Katie read me and gently placed a restraining hand on my arm. She realized what she'd done and quickly withdrew her hand as if she'd burned herself on a hot stove.

The kid, Kevin, was oblivious to all of this or at least acted that way. "You know they're going to jump you? I heard my brother talking about it," he said to me as he took another bight of his sandwich.

I ignored him and focused on trying to figure out why Katie pulled her hand back so fast and why it felt warm where she'd touched my arm. I looked at her again and was struck at how pretty she was. Her glasses didn't hide her big beautiful green eyes. They reminded me of a corn field in late spring. That calming green that made you feel good every time you saw it. When she smiled her whole face lit up like a sun beam breaking through a stained glass window. A sudden desire to make her smile seemed to be all I could think about.

Get a grip Scott. No way are you getting interested in a girl ever again. I'd learned my lesson well. The last thing I'd ever do was become interested in someone ever again.

## Chapter Four
<u>Katie</u>

It didn't take long for the wrath of the gods to descend on me like a ton of bricks. I hadn't made it ten feet out of the cafeteria before Nichole and Jennifer confronted me.

"What do you think you're doing skank?" Nichole asked. She stood in front of me with her hands on her hips like a bridge guarding troll. Jennifer hung back with a hungry look on her face. Large eyes, dilated pupils and a silly grin.

My stomach dropped and that old, familiar tightness in my chest returned. I hadn't felt this way since they took mom away. See this is what happens when you get involved.

I tried backing up but the rush of the lunch crowd kept pushing me forward. I was trapped like the rat they viewed me as. Why are girls like this? What did I ever do to them? We'd never talked. Yet here they were, acting like I was the second coming of the devil himself.

I had become un-cloaked, my invisibility lost forever. I was now firmly in everyone's awareness. There would be no more hiding in the shadows. A part of me had known this would happen when I sat across from Scott but I hadn't been able to stop myself.

Deciding to ignore the whole situation, I made a move to go around them. Nichole didn't agree with my plans and grabbed my arm. "I asked you a question bitch," she said with more venom than the situation deserved. I briefly wondered if she was more upset about me talking with Scott or with me trying to ignore her.

I looked at her hand. Strawberry red nails sparkled on my forearm. I hated being touched. Despised it with a deep passion. I flashed to another hand who had grabbed me there. A hard masculine hand that brought pain and shame. I stopped breathing and proceeded to lose it. I twisted my arm out of her grasp then stuck my face next to hers, eye to eye and said through gritted teeth. "If you ever touch me again I will scratch your eyes out and mail them to your mother. Do you understand?" All the color drained from her face as she tried to swallow.

Figuring she'd gotten the message, I turned and scooted past her. Making sure to bump into Jennifer who looked like she was about to pee her pants right there in the hallway. In all honesty I don't know who was more surprised, her or me.

Needless to say, Fourth and Fifth periods were rather tense. It seemed the quiet treatment had been expanded to include me.

Being ignored intentionally is different than being invisible. They made a point of catching my eye before turning their back. I laughed to myself; did they think I cared? It wouldn't have been a big deal. Easily ignored and forgotten. Until I got to my locker after fifth. Someone had kindly left me a message.

The words BITCH, SKANK, and SLUT were written in strawberry red nail polish all over the front metal door. The last T had run and dripped onto the floor like a sloppy exclamation point. The padlock and handle had been covered in the stuff and still looked wet.

Okay, this was getting serious; it was no longer business as usual, now it was personal. My face grew warm and I knew it'd gone beet red. The freshman girl next to me furrowed her brows in concern as she quietly closed her door and slowly backed away.

I stood there looking at my locker, trying to figure out what to do. No way was I going to cry, not here, not now. You've been through a lot worse Katie, I kept repeating to myself.

"You okay?" a deep voice said behind me. Why him? Of all the people in the universe. Why did he have to be here now? I turned to see Scott with a concerned look on his face. As if he actually gave a shit. I know I wasn't being very fare, this wasn't his fault. Unfortunately he could see the tears in my eyes and that made him the target of my anger.

"No of course I'm not okay. The people in this school are a bunch of assholes!" I said.

He laughed and said, "Really, I didn't know." He reached into the back pocket of his jeans and pulled out a snow white handkerchief, *"Who uses handkerchiefs anymore?"*.

Without saying anything he started wiping at the ugly words. They became a glaring garish red blasted against the yellow lockers. He swiped at the lock but it was a lost cause until it dried, even then I wouldn't be able to see the numbers. I wiped at my eyes while he had his back turned.

"Come on, I'll walk you to the library, you can probably get into your locker after school. Things should be dry by then." He gently touched my elbow to turn me and get me going. I flinched and drew away from him.

He immediately pulled his hand back and his brow creased in concern. I over-reacted again. Everything felt like it moved at a thousand miles a minute. He stuck his hand in his pocket and we made our way to the library.

It felt strange walking next to someone. He caught me having to skip to keep up and slowed to match my stride. I didn't notice what the other people were doing; I even started to forget about my locker. I kept thinking about the boy next to me, sneaking a look from behind the hair in my eyes. He caught me and smiled all the while keeping his hands in his pocket.

Holding my library door open he smiled and motioned me in with a flamboyant flourish. He gently touched my lower back making me visibly shiver. He immediately returned his hands to his pocket and shot me an apologetic smile.

Placing his books on his center table, he turned and tossed the now pink handkerchief into the trash can. My heart skipped a beat, I felt guilty. He'd ruined his handkerchief for me. What if it was important, had it been his father's? I couldn't stand it if it had belonged to his dad. I'd give anything to have something of my dad's, - whoever he was - the thought that I might have caused Scott to lose something important made my stomach knot up in a ball.

He wasn't perturbed as he swung a leg over his regular chair and plopped down. Pulling out his book he focused and drifted into a different world. Like I said earlier, there are different kinds of being ignored, some are most definitely worse.

I stared at him and for the first time in my life wished I was pretty, I wanted him to look at me and not be able to look away.

"What are you reading?" I asked. Unwilling to let our moment go. He looked at me then back at his book.

"History of the English Speaking People, Volume two. By Winston Churchill" He answered and laughed at the look of disbelief on my face. I mean come on, the guy was a nerd, handkerchiefs, history books, holding doors open. Definitely a died in the flannel nerd If it hadn't been for those wide shoulders and arms the size of railroad ties.

He sheepishly shrugged. "It was my dad's. I'm reading all of his books. I started last year and I've only made it to the C's."

"Is it any good?"

"Yeah it is. It's sort of neat reading ancient history from a famous politician's point of view. He sees things a little differently than your normal historian." He shrugged his shoulders again and returned to reading. "Besides, the man can write."

Wow, nerd to the ninth degree.

We spent the period talking about books. It surprised me how easy he was to talk to. I didn't feel the normal anxiety like I felt whenever I talked one on one. Especially with boys. He told me about how his dad had caught him reading late at night in bed with a flashlight. But hadn't been upset. The next day his dad had returned from his grandfather's farm with all of his old Science Fiction books that he'd loved as a boy.

My heart sort of flipped when he mentioned that he now slept in his dad's old room and all those books were back on their original shelf. I wondered what it would be like to have that kind of dad. The kind that shared your love of something, that you could talk to, ask questions of.

It was nice to talk to someone. When the bell rang I jumped in surprise, I'd forgotten all about my locker. Scott gathered his books and glanced at the front door then back to me. I think he wanted to say something. He hesitated then seemed to change his mind when Mattie stepped in. He smiled and said. "Take care Katie, see you tomorrow."

I watched him leave and my heart fluttered. I pulled out a handy wipe and used it to retrieve his handkerchief from the trash.

.o0o.

The next morning my psychedelic locker waited for me in its usual place. I found myself walking slower and slower as I approached. But there leaning next to it, his arms folded stood my gentle giant in his red Letterman Jacket. He smiled when he saw me and pushed off, holding huge lock snips. I furrowed my brow in question. He ignored the query and handed me a small bag then cut my lock off as if he was cutting a piece of paper. He turned back to smile at me again but wouldn't answer my questioning look. For the first time I noticed a small chip on one of his front teeth. You wouldn't normally see it, not unless you were looking hard.

He opened my locker and clucked his tongue at the neatness, shaking his head back and forth while he chuckled. I wanted to dive in and hide my box of handy wipe packets but he stood in the way and I could no more move him than I could have shifted the Rockies.

Pulling a screwdriver out of his back pocket he started removing my locker number then the obnoxious door itself. I stepped back and folded my arms. I could wait, he better have a great explanation. People were staring as they walked by; we were definitely not being ignored now.

When he'd unscrewed the last screw he reached down and picked up a fresh locker door from the floor. I hadn't seen it there.

"Where did you get that?" I said.

"Don't ask. The less you know the less you can get in trouble."

My stomach rolled over and I had to fight to hold down a giggle. Was he really doing this for me? Why?

Once he finished, he retrieved the bag and the lock inside. Carefully reading the combo from the package, he opened the lock, put it in place and gave me the combo. Giving me one last smile he picked up the old door and started down the hall like he had nothing better to do.

"Wait Scott, I mean, thanks, but what's the use. They'll just ruin this one."

"No they won't," he said and held out his phone to show me a picture of a car, a silver hatchback. The special touch was the text in Strawberry Red. "Nice car Nichol, shame if something happened to it."

The man was a genius.

## Chapter Five
### Scott

The four of us were sitting in our regular table in the middle of the cafeteria. I dropped my fork onto my tray, "How do you screw up spaghetti? How hard can it be? You open a can, boil the noodles. I hate it when they do this. It should be against the law or something." Everybody ignored my rant and concentrated on their meals.

"If you couldn't tell, spaghetti is his favorite," Mattie said in an aside to Katie.

The buzz in the room suddenly stopped when Danny Carrs walked in. It sounded like the crickets going silent at sunrise. An eerie calm that prickled at the skin.

I knew it had to happen sometime, but the knife to the gut was still a shock. He wore a white cast on his right wrist and my skanky ex-girlfriend on his left. To tell you the truth she looked good which only shoved the knife in a little farther. She wore a short pleated black skirt and a pretty pink fitted shirt. She obviously went for that conservative, innocent; butter wouldn't melt in her mouth look.

She scanned the room until she located me. We locked glares for a moment until she smiled the sweetest, most venomous smile ever seen in this part of the state. I swear it was laced with acid. Gina pulled on Danny's arm to make him aware of me.

Danny glanced my way without an expression. Panned over my companions, finally coming to rest on Katie. His eyebrows rose for a moment before he turned back to his friends. We obviously were not worth worrying about.

I forced myself to focus on my meal. Glancing over I caught Katie looking at me with a concerned expression.

"What?" I asked rather sharply.

"Nothing, Nothing." She said holding up her hands before I could bight her head off.

"I hear they had to go back in to adjust the pins," Kevin said referring to Danny's hand. "How'd you break it anyway? The story is that you held it down and hit it with a hammer."

"Kevin!" Mattie gasped.

"What?" he said innocently but the twinkle in his eye led me to believe he knew exactly what he was doing.

"Let's change the subject, I hear you fell in P.E. while running around the track," Mattie said to Kevin.

"I didn't fall. Ryan Jennings tripped me. On purpose."

"What," I said. "I thought this crap hadn't spread to the freshman class. You guys told me everything was all right." My guts turned over thinking about Mattie being hassled.

"Not everything's about you big guy." Kevin said. Like I said earlier, bull's balls. "I didn't let Ryan cheat off my test in sixth grade." He said. "We've been butting heads ever since."

There was no way of telling if it was the truth and I couldn't think of anything that might change their minds so let the matter drop and returned to looking at the popular table. Gina was draped all over Danny, her arm around his shoulder looking up at him with adoring eyes. It was funny when you think about it. He used to joke about clingy girls; they drove him up the wall. He'd say they looked like sucking lampreys hanging off a shark.

Katie coughed, interrupting my wool gathering. I dragged my eyes off the cute couple across the way and focused on those around me.

"What are you reading?" I asked her. Within minutes we were deep into disagreement about Hawthorn's influences on today's literature. Mattie and Kevin whispered to each other and giggled about something. I let it go without comment. Mattie seemed to have lost her need to be quiet. I did notice that she had a habit of letting Kevin finish his thought before jumping in. The guy had to be commended.

After we'd finished I followed Katie to the trash cans and made a deposit. Katie and I'd gotten into the habit of walking together to our shared fourth period class. A couple of weeks ago I had barely registered the fact that we were in the same classroom. Now I found myself feeling better whenever I was around her. Our discussions about books, the way she'd smile at me from behind her bangs whenever I said something semi-intelligent. I liked to hear her laugh, it had a throaty rumble that sent a chill up my spine. Occasionally her eyes would widen as if she was surprised to find herself enjoying life.

She held her books to her chest as we walked towards class. "Are you worried, I mean with Danny being back. You said they'd wait for him to come back before jumping you," Katie asked, looking up at me with puppy eyes.

I chuckled. "If he does, I'll just threaten to scratch his eyes out and mail them to his mom."

She turned a sexy red and lowered her head. I don't think she was used to friendly teasing. It felt different having a girl for a friend. Gina and I were never really friends. I never teased her and we didn't talk about much unless we had deep philosophical discussions about hair styles or who should be going out with whom. Mostly Gina had the discussion. I listened.

It came as a lightning bolt from the blue, I hadn't enjoyed being with her. I'd liked the idea of thinking that someone as beautiful as her could be with me, that and the fact that she had me in a constant state of sexual excitement.

Danny and his clique of zombies were waiting for us when we rounded the corner. They were bunched in the center of the hall, each of them paired up. This was no longer a guy thing, their girlfriends were in full support of Gina. Danny held my conniving ex's hand and smiled at me with a gleam that let me know he was sure of himself. Being backed up by six football players obviously helped his confidence.

Katie gasped and halted in place. Six to one, I could have taken two maybe three, but six was too much even for me. I gently pushed Katie behind me. The protective juices had kicked into high gear. My heart skipped a beat when I thought about her seeing what was going to happen. These types of fights weren't like in the movies. They were ugly with a lot of blood and pain.

I could sense how she hated violence or confrontation. I didn't want her to see me get my ass kicked by six guys. For some reason it was important to me that she be impressed.

I returned Danny's smile and stared him in the eye letting him know exactly what I thought of him. He had the grace to momentarily look embarrassed but it passed quickly and he was back to his cocky normal self.

Nicole giggled nervously and Tommy coughed into his hand. I glanced at Gina and shook my head, what had I ever seen in this girl. How had I let myself be misled by fluttering eyelashes and a well-rounded hip? It pissed me off, being such a dunce.

I looked back at Danny and said, "So, I see you've got your own personal lamprey." Gina frowned in confusion, but Danny knew what I meant, I swear he wanted to drop her hand right there and then.

All activity had come to a screeching halt in the hallway. Every student froze in place to see what was going on. Within moments we were surrounded. Danny and I continued to stare at each other. The air grew thicker and thicker with tension as if a mist of oppression had settled over the hallway. Both of us waiting for the other to make the first move.

"You won't get another chance for a sucker punch," Danny said. Obviously he'd decided to play this as if it was all my fault, he had to try and save face. That's what happens when you're on top of the social stratosphere; you had to constantly manipulate perception to stay there.

I laughed, "That wasn't a sucker punch that was a rat-bastard punch. But that's what happens when a guy screws his best friend's girl behind his back." The crowd collectively inhaled. I finally had that pithy statement, here in front of a bunch of rabid idiots.

"He shoots, he scores." Someone said. Several people laughed.

Danny flinched before squaring his shoulder and cursing under his breath. "Hey that's not how it went down." As a comeback it was pretty lame. Someone laughed, trying to show support but overall it landed like a dud and Danny knew it.

Dropping Gina's hand he hunched his shoulders and prepared to launch himself. I could see it deep in his eyes. He hated me with an overriding passion. I'd ruined his season. Taken potential glory from him. I'd made him look small. Most of all, he felt guilty and knew I'd never forgive him. He wanted to hurt me, believe me I knew how he felt. I wanted to pound his head into the ground and stomp on the pile.

My heart raced and my hands clenched into fists as I prepared for his charge. I'd let him make the first move. Fighting protocol demanded it, he had the physical support of his friends and I had hit him first last time. But I wouldn't let him get in deep. The first chance I got I was taking him down hard.

"What's going on here?" Mr. Thompson said as he forced his way through the crowd. The kids were slow to move out of his way, obviously disappointed to see their fun being interrupted. He glanced at Danny and myself and immediately stepped between us. "Don't you people have some place to be?" He said staring at the crowd

## Certain Rules

daring any of them to contradict him. "Anyone here when the bell rings will be in detention for a week, now get to class," he shouted

The tension started to ease and I thought I might be able to get out of this. At least for now. Danny saw his opportunity creeping away and charged me. Mr. Thompson put a hand on his chest holding him back while his friends grabbed his shoulders.

"Not now, not here." John said.

Danny looked down at the teachers hand on his chest and seemed to come to the realization of where he was at. He relaxed and stepped back.

"Later James, he sneered.

The observers started to disperse, they knew nothing much more was likely to happen with a teacher there. The students reluctantly moved away and started commenting to each other about what had just happened. There were quite a few comments about my Rat-bastard quip. One of the younger boys mentioned how a broken wrist would have been worth it for a chance to be with Gina Woods.

Every muscle tensed as adrenalin pumped through my body. I kept my eye on Danny, waiting for his next move. I felt Katie's gentle hand force my fist open as she slipped her hand into mine. "Come on Scott, let's go," she said as she tried to pull me away.

Mr. Thompson relaxed a little when he noticed everyone dispensing and turned back to Danny and myself. He shook his head as if he was disappointed in us. Taking a breath he said, "Scott, please come with me." He reached out and gently grabbed my shoulder and turned me away from the confrontation. "You to Rivers," he said to Katie. Including her in our departure.

He escorted us into an empty room, his shoulders slumping as we entered. "I won't waste our time talking about what just happened," he said. "I wanted to ask you if it is true that you've lost your scholarship offer to Nebraska," he said. It felt like a knife stab to the heart every time I thought about what'd been lost.

Katie hissed through her teeth and held her hand to her lips. "You didn't tell me," Katie said, back handing my shoulder then looked shocked at what she'd done. Mr. Thompson caught it and smiled.

I laughed. "It wasn't a surprise, Coach Carlson told me he was going to make sure it happened. The letter just confirmed something I already knew was going to happen." Okay, I lied a little. The letter yesterday had been like a dagger to the heart. I had secretly hoped they'd change their minds and not do it. But the paper had confirmed my worst fear as my dreams dissolved into a warm puddle.

Mr. Thompson shook his head and crooked his mouth in disdain. I don't know who he was more upset at, Coach Carlson, Nebraska, or me. "I'm sure other schools would be willing," he said.

"No it has to be Nebraska, Mom and Dad went there, they met there. I was born at the university hospital while they were attending. If I go to college, it will be there.

He nodded as if he understood. I'd forgotten that he knew my dad. They'd gone to this very school together. The way he looked whenever I mentioned Coach Carlson's

# Certain Rules

name and Grandfathers statement about Dad and Carlson getting into a fight made me wonder if it had been Mr. Thompson that dad had been protecting. I was sure it was. Maybe that was why Mr. Thompson was looking out for me. Years after he died dad was still watching over me. A warm sense of well-being washed through me. And the knife wound to the heart eased off a little.

"Have you thought about an academic scholarship? Your GPA is close enough that you could probably qualify? A little work this year and you could guarantee it. You'd have to hurry and get the applications in. I'm sure Ms. Rivers could help." He said, smiling at Katie who was nodding vehemently. And suddenly I knew Katie would help without question. There didn't have to be anything in it for her, she would help because that was the type of person she was.

"I don't know, I hadn't really thought about it. Without football, there's not much reason to go."

"Well think about it, I know your dad and mom would want you to go to college. He always used to say it was a favorite time in his life."

Katie touched my elbow to get my attention and was still nodding vehemently. "I think you should Scott, don't let them get away with this."

"What about you Ms. Rivers?" Mr. Thompson asked.

Her eyes widened like a deer in the headlights. She didn't like being the center of attention. "I don't know, I hadn't thought about it."

Her answer surprised me. Katie seemed like a natural for college. Not only book smart, but she got life.

Understood what was important and what wasn't. I knew she was hiding some deep dark secret. The conservative, baggy clothes, the hiding behind her hair. A wound so deep that if it opened she might explode. My heart went out to her, but whatever happened shouldn't keep her from going to college.

She struggled with being put on the spot and shrugged her shoulders; she didn't have a good answer.

"Tell you what, we can help each other fill out the forms. What's the worst that could happen? They tell us no," I said.

Mr. Thompson smiled with a self-satisfied grin, he' done his good deed for the day. Katie's eyes clouded over in concern, there was something she didn't want to face, and this was going to force her to.

## Chapter Six
### Katie

Aunt Jenny's house was immaculate as always. I don't know why she worried about it. No one ever came for a visit. It really didn't bother me. I like things clean, but I always felt uncomfortable there. Always afraid that I'd put something out of place, leave a glass on the table or knock a lamp over. The furniture wasn't covered in plastic, but still.

Aunt Jenny hadn't known I existed until last year. Nor I her. My mom hadn't ever told me about her family. I'd always assumed she was an orphan.

What hurt the most was knowing that my grandmother had died six months before I found out about my extended family. She'd left this house to her daughter. The same house my aunt and my mom had grown up in. In fact, I slept in their old room.

The mantel clock quietly ticked away the hour. Obviously Aunt Jenny was out. She worked as a checker at the local grocery store. Her shift was earlier in the day so she should have been home.

Shrugging my shoulders I went into my room and started on my homework. I tried to keep the confrontation with Danny Carrs from leaking into my thoughts and failed miserably. The tension had been as thick as spaghetti sauce. Gina looked like she'd won the lottery. Her silly grin spread across her face and her eye lit up like a car's high beams.

Danny Carrs on the other hand had been all 'No big deal' until he saw me. For a moment his eyebrows had scrunched up and he shot me a stare of pure hate. It had hit me like a physical blow. Just as fast it was gone, to be replaced by a crap eating grin. Like he didn't have a care in the world. It was only then that he'd focused on Scott.

Giving up on my homework I plopped onto my bed and folded my hands under my head and studied my ceiling. Counting bumps and trying to remember what it felt like to hold Scott's hand. Anything to delay the flood of emotions I knew were about to overwhelm me.

I had to admit to myself how scared I'd been with the whole Danny thing. I wasn't frightened for myself. I felt petrified though about what might happen to Scott. There were six of them. Then to find out he had lost his scholarship. What could Nebraska be thinking; the guy was a mountain who ruled the football field.

This had to be tearing him apart. He'd never show it. The man refused to let anyone see he had problems. Keeping everything inside, to be handled by him. He never complained. Never put Gina down, not really. Most people would have whined and torn her apart. Instead, he took it all onto those massive shoulders and pushed through.

I know I had put the scholarship applications issues off by thinking about Scott. I liked thinking about him. I did a lot of that lately.

My mind kept conjuring up images. Scott reading in my library. Scott walking down the hall with his books in his left hand. Wearing his red and white letterman jacket. The smooth and graceful way he moved. It reminded me of a Budweiser Clydesdale. Those horses always looked so smooth, so together, like nothing could ever hurt them. I knew it wasn't true. But you had to admire somebody like that.

His thick rich brown eyes haunted me. They had a way of looking deep into my soul, trapping me in place. There were little specks of gold that fired off whenever he laughed. Kevin's jokes made them light up, making me tingle all over.

This is crazy Katie, I thought. Do not get interested in this boy. He isn't over Gina yet. The stares he'd laid on her today were not casual glances. They were the looks of someone seriously in love. All glassy eyed and far way. Besides, if he ever found out about me I'd die. Simply cease to exist. That thought set my stomach into chaos changing the nice butterflies into full blown buzzards. Which brought up the whole scholarship issue.

If I applied I'd have to give them information about my parents, or my mom at least. They would want my whole high school history. No way would anyone give thousands of dollars to somebody whose mom sat in a California prison. So why even try. *Because you told him you would.*

I could kick myself for agreeing to Mr. Thompson. He was quickly becoming my least favorite teacher. I'd have to find a way to avoid the entire subject. No way was I letting Scott discover my secrets.

.oOo.

The next morning I decided to adjust my wardrobe a little. I wasn't invisible anymore. There was no longer a requirement to hide behind my cloths. Of course I wasn't going to go all slutty like the other girls. Simple Jeans and a fitted shirt with my hair pulled back with barrettes.

Scott smiled when he saw me first period. He didn't say anything about my outfit though. The smile would have to be enough.

I ruined our daily library interlude later by my pretending to be busy the entire period. The thought of him asking about the scholarship packages sent chills from my toes to my ears.

We'd both gotten through the day without any serious problems. The popular squad was obviously biding their time. The last thing I wanted to do was ruin it by begging off on the scholarship package.

The final bell rang and I sighed in relief. I'd gotten through without any mention of college. I looked at him and my muscles froze. Scott wasn't leaving. He continued to read his book occasionally glancing at the clock over the front door. Was he waiting for me to finish my work so we could do the packages? Where was Mattie? My heart started to pound.

Fifteen minutes after final bell a soft flop of a closing book had me checking out what was going on. He put his stuff away and looked at me with a smile.

"Mattie's got a freshman girls' basketball game."

It took a lot of effort, but I was able to stop my shoulders from slumping with relief and offered a small prayer of thanks. I don't know if I believe in god or not, right then though, I was pretty sure somebody was looking out for me.

"I didn't know she was on the team," I said.

What kind of person did that make me? Granted, I seemed to be tuned into everything Scott said. I reminded myself to make sure to pay attention to Mattie.

"Yea, this is their first game and she's pretty jazzed."

"Do you think she'd mind me coming to the game," I asked. My face flushed. Did I just invite myself to a basketball game with Scott James? What would he think? Would he think I liked him that way? Come on Katie, it's only a basketball game; you didn't ask him to the prom. My heart raced and my stomach turned over waiting for his reply.

"Sure, she'd love it," he said as if nothing special had just happened.

Scott held the gym door open for me then gently placed his hand on the small of my back to usher me inside. A gentle chill spread up my spine. The feeling didn't go away when his hand dropped. What's more, I didn't flinch.

The gym was almost empty and smelt like new floor wax and old socks. This place had way too many memories of awful P.E. classes. Only the center section of bleachers had been pulled out with six people scattered on the wooden benches. I guessed freshman girls' basketball is not a real popular draw.

Kevin Hays sat in the middle of the stands. You had to give the kid credit, he was fully invested. Scott held my elbow as we climbed the stands. Did he think I was a clumsy idiot? *Relax Katie, he's a gentleman. It's not all about you".* I thought.

I sat between the both of them and tried to concentrate on the game. Occasionally my shoulder or knee would brush against Scott sending an electric charge throughout my body. He had to be aware of what happened. How could he not be? I mean it was like the ozone layer was set on fire whenever we touched.

Mattie started at point guard and controlled the game like a small general. Kevin couldn't stop smiling and was her biggest cheerleader. Every time she scored all three of us would stand and yell "Go Tigers, Go Mattie". She'd look at us and sheepishly smile while trying to hide a flaming red face.

The game went well and I had a great time. Kevin got Scott to do the three person wave. Some of the others bystanders thought we were crazy. I didn't care. It was fun not being invisible.

The Tigers won by twenty points, thanks in large part to Mattie. The teams ran off to the locker rooms after the final whistle. There was a momentary awkwardness as I tried to figure out what I was supposed to do next. Did I wait to congratulate Mattie? Did I leave? Kevin saved me by announcing his attention to wait.

She ran from the locker room a few minutes later. Her wet pony tail hopping back and forth and a huge grin plastered across her lips. She gave Scott a hug then turned and hugged me, thanking us for coming. Letting go she made a move as if to hug Kevin but thought better about it and pulled back. "Thanks for coming. I was surprised to see you guys here. Your cheers were driving the other team crazy."

Kevin kept his smile and fought to hide his disappointment as he stuck his hands in his back pockets.

Another awkward moment settled over us until Mattie asked her brother, "Are you taking me for pizza like you promised." Scott smiled and nodded.

"What kind of pizza do you guys like?" Mattie said to Kevin and I. "I prefer just extra cheese, Scott likes them with everything. Please help me here; I never get it my way."

My heart skipped and I shot a glance towards Scott, did he mean for us to tag along or had his sister just put him in an untenable position. His face was its normal impassive, emotional blank face. He was impossible to read and it drove me up the wall. The man didn't let anything come across. Not unless he wanted you to know.

He shifted from foot to foot and said, "You can get what you want when you start buying. But with the four of us, we can probably get both." His smile at Mattie's glowing response said how much he loved his kid sister.

I hesitated at his truck. Mattie opened the door and motioned for me to sit in the middle. I would be squeezed next to Scott. My heart got a lot of exercise thinking about it. I slid in while Kevin jumped in the bed. I know he wasn't supposed to sit back there. It was one of those rules that people around here ignored. The cops didn't enforce it because they thought it was a stupid law. They'd all grown up doing the same thing.

The faded paint of Scott's black and white F150 made it appear older than him. For all I knew it might have been. The insides smelt like old leather and fresh hay and all Scott. I wanted to sink in and never leave. The engine sprang into a deep rumble when he turned the keys. He shifted into first gear and his hand accidently touched my knee. My leg jumped and hit the radio. The music shifted from classic rock to a country station.

Mattie laughed. "No one's allowed to change the station," she said, shaking her head. "It's all he ever listens too."

My brow raised in a questioning look. Obviously this was a sore point between them.

"It was the last station dad had programmed in." He said shooting Mattie a withering stare.

I regretfully moved my legs out of his way. I'm sure there is a rule somewhere that says you're supposed to stay out of the driver's way when he shifts gear. It was a rule I desperately wanted to ignore.

We piled out at Joe's Pizzeria, the best and only pizza joint in town. Mattie punched Kevin's shoulder for some reason then ran inside to pick the best spot. Kevin of course pretended to chase her. When I looked over, Scott frowned and shook his head at their antics. "What?" I asked.

"I don't know if I'm ready for her being interested in boys."

"She's fifteen, believe me, she's been interested for a while."

"I know," he said continuing to frown. "But this is different."

"He's a good guy, she'd be lucky to get him."

"No guy's good enough," he said pulling the door open for me. "But your right, he is a good guy, she could do a lot worse."

Mattie and Kevin were sitting next to each other in a back booth. Their heads together as they fought over the best crust. I guess I had to sit next to Scott. Correction got to sit next to him. He always made me feel tiny and feminine.

This had sort of turned into a double date. Mattie's face glowed with pleasure and I wondered if she'd set this up on purpose. Was it her way of spending time with Kevin or was she trying to set me up with Scott. My stomach started revolving like an old fashioned record when I thought about her doing that. He wasn't ready, and was most definitely not interested in dating me. Besides. I didn't date. Rule number one, don't get involved. Remember?

A thousand thoughts flew threw my brain. I was so lost in my own little world that I didn't see the waitress approach. She flashed Scott a smile and I wanted to rip her lips off. *What, was I invisible?* Hold on Katie, I thought. This was not the way things should be going.

Pulling myself together and ignoring the electric buzz coming off of Scott. I focused back on the others and got Mattie into a discussion about the game.

The pizza was great and the conversation better. Unlike the cafeteria.

It was nice to be part of a group. Is this what normal people felt? I liked it, the laughter, the warm feeling of belonging. They'd welcomed me and treated me as if I was normal. I'd never let them know the truth; I couldn't stand the idea of them being disappointed in me.

Those thoughts led me into thinking about the man next to me. I knew I didn't have a chance in him being interested in me. But still. I fanaticized what would it be like for this special man to find me special. For a short while I forgot about my past, the pain and shame were washed away and I felt wonderful. Life was great.

There is a rule, I think they call it Murphy's Law. Things that can go wrong will go wrong. That was my life to the ninth degree. We had almost finished when the door opened and the leaders of the popular clique entered. Laughing and joking like they didn't have a care in the world. John and Nicole were holding hands. She'd dressed in skin tight jeans and a low cut top. A fashion statement that only a few girls could pull off, unfortunately she was one of them. Gina looked gorgeous as always. A classy skirt and sweater set that enhanced her perfect figure.

I snuck a peak at Scott to see how he was taking her entrance. He didn't see her, his eyes were totally focused on Danny. The group noticed us and froze in place. They had a hasty conversation before selecting a booth as far away as possible.

Mattie stopped talking in mid-sentence. The light hearted, happy feeling had been washed away as if someone had dumped a bucket of cold water over everything.

We finished up. Scott left a generous tip and paid the bill at the cashier while the rest of us made our way outside. I hung back. No way would I leave him in there alone. He cast a glance back towards them then joined me at the door. Flashing me a smile, trying to reassure me that everything was okay.

Clouds had moved in while we were inside, casting everything into gray shadows. A cool wind ruffled my hair. I was glad I'd pulled it back. There were some benefits for using barrettes.

We didn't make it all the way to his truck before the restaurant door slammed open. John and Danny rushed outside followed by the two females of the evil quartet.

"Where you going bastard? Running away again." John yelled across the parking lot.

Scott slammed to a halt and hunched his shoulders as if someone had shoved a knife into his back. My heart raced and my hands got all clammy. Why couldn't they leave us alone? I prayed that Scott would keep going. That he'd shake it off and ignore them. We were all getting so good at ignoring them. But no, he couldn't do that.

Kevin jumped out of the back of the truck and Mattie joined him as they walked toward us to help. The fearsome foursome continued towards us from the other side. Four on four I thought. I knew who I'd attack if necessary. Gina Woods was going down if I got the chance. I wouldn't mind leaving scratch marks across that flawless face.

Look at me, I thought. Two weeks ago I was invisible. Working very hard to stay that way. And now I'm thinking about pulling some girls hair out at the root.

Kevin stepped up to stand on the other side of Scott and Mattie filled out the end. Scott looked at Kevin and shook his head and let out a little short laugh. A scene from the movie O.K. Corral flashed through my mind. We looked like a bunch of cowboys facing off. I had to stop from chuckling. It was all so stupid.

John made a move towards us and my stomach brought me back to reality. This could get really dirty real fast. I found myself holding my breath waiting for Scott to react.

"John, what would you have done if you'd found Nicole with her feet in the air and Danny buried between them?" Scott said as if he really wanted to know.

John's face turned white. He looked like he'd been doused with a fire hose. All the steam had been let out. He hesitated a moment and said, "I wouldn't have ruined our season, man."

"Doesn't that make you feel special," I said to Nicole, loving the way her face scrunched up as if I'd slapped that silly smile right off it. John looked back at her then at Danny. I could tell he was real confused.

Gina's face was lit up like a Christmas tree, the thought of boys fighting over her had animated her like she was on fire. It bugged the hell out of me, this was all her fault. She'd ruined a lifelong friendship. Destroyed the schools chance for football glory. And demolished Scott's heart.

My insides hardened into a rock, it'd been a long time since I'd hated someone this much. But I also realized that there wasn't a thing I could do to her that would make her feel as bad as she'd made everyone else feel. Imagine going through life like that, so self-centered that nothing could affect you.

The tension had been let out of the situation. Scott's question had taken the steam out of John and Danny wouldn't make a move without his backup. I needed to get everyone out of there before he changed his mind. "Come on you guys, I've got to get home," I said.

Scott seemed to accept it and walked with us back to the truck. I could feel the cold stares boring into our backs. There weren't any more snide comments though. Scott's question had changed things.

We dropped Kevin off first. He hopped out and came to Mattie's window. She rolled the window down and smiled at him. He stuck his head in and thanked Scott for the pizza, assuring him that the next time the food would be on him. I thought how smart could you be. He was already laying the ground work for next time. Scott chuckled and said "Sure, anytime."

Kevin turned back to Mattie with a huge smile. "Thanks for asking me out Mattie, I had a great time."

Mattie's smile dropped as she choked on a reply, sputtering and hemming. Seeing her discomfort made Kevin's smile grow even more. Then he shocked all three of us by leaning in and kissing her on the lips. It wasn't a long wet sloppy kiss, but definitely long enough for her to pull away which she complete did not do.

Mattie froze in place, her face in shock while Kevin sauntered across his front yard like a man who'd just conquered Mt Everest. Slowly her face split out in a huge smile to be replaced by a deep frown.

"What's wrong," I asked.

Her frown had changed into an angry scowl. "He finally kisses me and it's through a car window and right in front of my brother. That's not how I imagined my first kiss would go."

Scott and I laughed. She was really upset. I leaned over and whispered. "Other than that, how was it?

She thought for a moment and then smiled again. "Good, very good."

## Chapter Seven

### Scott

There should be a rule that little sisters don't grow up. No, it should be a law or something. Kevin and Mattie's kiss the other day was bugging me to no end. I tried shifting my mind away be thinking about my ex best friend.

Today at lunch I actually felt sorry for Danny. Before Kevin and Mattie had joined us, Katie caught me staring at the lovely couple. I couldn't avoid it. They drew me like moths to a flame.

"She'll be pregnant before graduation," Katie said with a raised eyebrow, daring me to contradict her.

"How do you know," I said. Surprised at how little her statement hurt.

"She has her claws in too deep. He's her path out. I bet she's mapped out four years at college then on to the NFL. What's worse, she thinks she deserves it all."

I laughed, "Boy, she's in for a rude awakening."

"What do you mean," Katie said.

"He'll never make the NFL, he's not good enough and isn't willing to put in the work necessary. He's always been surrounded by a very good team. Always been a big fish in a very little pond. I don't think he'll start at the college level, let alone make the Pro's."

Katie shook her head as she watched them. "I want to be there when she finds out."

"I wouldn't want to be in Danny's shoes for anything." I said with a shudder. Thinking about what kind of hell Gina would make of his life made me shiver as if someone had walked over my grave.

"Do you mean that," Katie asked in surprise.

"What, that I'm glad not to be in his shoes. Yes, I guess I do."

"Sleeping with Gina Woods. I thought it was every boys dream."

"Yea. Well, I've grown up a lot in the last couple of weeks. You know, -- I don't think I even liked her, I wanted her. Don't get me wrong, I liked the way she made me feel, like I was important. Maybe as if I was a little better because I had Gina Woods as my girlfriend. You know?" She nodded in understanding. "But we were never friends. Do you believe that? We were with each other for six months and I can't ever remember asking her to help with something. Not like she'd have given it. I can't even tell you her favorite desert."

Katie stared at her half sandwich the entire time I rambled. I could never tell what she thought. She looked up smiling and said, "Mine's cheesecake, just in case anyone ever asks."

Chuckling, I started in on my second burger.

"Six months, -- and you guys never —"Katie asked, her face growing an attractive pink shade of embarrassed.

It took me a moment to understand what she was asking. My back went up, where did she get the right to ask such a personal question? *She got the right by standing next to you for a month while you went through this crap*, I answered myself and shrugged my shoulders.

"A gentleman doesn't talk about a lady, but since she's no lady, why not. No, never."

Katie's eyebrows rose high on her forehead in surprise. I guess she hadn't believed the rumors and needed me to confirm them.

"Don't get me wrong, there were –times—before Gina, girls who were willing, well, a girl anyway."

"Who," she asked with a mountain of interest in her eyes.

"I can't believe I'm talking about this stuff with you. No, I'm not going to tell you. She is a lady, and deserves my discretion."

"Hmp, Tell me if I guess." She paused for a second and looked the popular group over. "Nichol, no she's been with John forever and you're not the poaching kind. I know, how about Janice Cooper, I here she's always willing."

"Put the claws away Katie, they're unbecoming." She flashed me a smile. "You don't know her, she graduated before you got here. What about you, are you going to tell me about your love life."

It was like I'd hit the off button. The color drained from her face and she stared at her lap. Shaking her head she mumbled something about having to go. She stood and was half way across the room before I could register what was going on. She almost ran Mattie and Kevin over in her efforts to get away.

Mattie looked after her and then back at me. "What did you do now!" she demanded.

"I don't know Mattie, but whatever it was, it was pretty bad."

Another rule I'd make would be that girls as sweet and cute as Katie should never be hurt. Nobody should ever be hurt like that. I don't know what happened but it was bad. It wasn't some simple heart break. Something had scarred her to the core.

Sometimes she'd look off into distance, her face scrunched in pain. I'd try to pull her out of it but could never make her forget entirely. The only time I'd come close was at Joe's Pizzeria. She'd been so happy. Her smile were priceless. It made me want to get it back somehow.

.oOo.

Katie

New rule Katie, I thought as I rushed for the girl's bathroom. No joking with Scott about his love life. Better yet, no talking with Scott period. My heart raced out of control and my eyes threatened to explode into tears. How could I let this happen? He must think I'm crazy. No, I just confirmed I was crazy.

The door couldn't get out of my way fast enough as I slammed into it. The jibber jabber of the occupants came to an instant halt when I rushed in. Their eyes as wide as coffee cups and smiles as big as snakes when they saw my distress. I didn't care what they saw or what they thought as I crashed into a stall and threw up my lunch.

So much for being invisible. I couldn't believe I'd allowed myself to get into this state. I'd lost situational awareness as the military geeks said. Scott had been so cute when I teased him, my insides had gotten all mushy when he talked about himself. The fact that he might ask me questions had never crossed my mind. For a moment we'd been normal teenagers teasing each other. The next moment my guts had been torn out as visions of my hell had flooded through me.

What was I going to do now? I'd never be able to face him again. Oh sweet god, I thought. We have Mr. Thompson together next period. Well this definitely meant I'd be skipping that class. I had to.

The girls outside the stall were giggling, making jokes about morning sickness and about worshiping at the porcelain goddess. I so didn't care. May they all contact scabies or fatal flatulence in church.

"Katie, are you okay?" Mattie said as she slowly opened the door to my little safe haven. That was it, all that was necessary to push me over the edge. My body began shaking as deep throaty sobs burst out of me like small explosions. I slumped to the side and curled into a ball with my face buried in my knees. Mattie had sounded so concerned. Such a good friend. What would she think if she knew the truth?

I knew what happened wasn't my fault. That I had done what I had to do. But my friends wouldn't see it that way. Especially him. Scott was so perfect, other than those occasional violent tendencies. He was supper intelligent, larger than a small mountain, stronger than a beefed up bear and so sweet he could put a person into a diabetic coma.

I tried to catch my breath while Mattie squatted next to me and brushed my hair out of my eyes.

Giving her a weak smile. I tried pushing myself out of my hole. She smiled encouraging me the best she could.

Shooting the outside crowd a nasty look that was enough to get them to back off for a moment, I pushed my way to the sinks, not caring about those dumb enough not to get out of my way.

"Is there anything I can do?" Mattie asked as she rubbed my back. Her touch didn't bother me, I found it soothing. Maybe I could get over this. Could I put this behind me? Every fiber of my soul wanted to.

A vision of Scott rubbing my back flashed in my mind. I wanted so bad to bury my face in his shoulder. What would it be like to let someone hold me? Only if I could do it without him knowing why.

Mattie smiled at me in the mirror, obviously happy to see me looking like I'd regained some semblance of semi-control. The face that looked back at me appeared to have been run over by a lawn mower. My red eyes announced to everyone that I'd been balling my eyes out. White blotches of pale pasty skin made me look like a poorly made quilt. To top it off my hair had become a tangled mess. A look that was not conducive to remaining invisible.

"What's going on Katie, is there anything I can do?" Mattie asked.

A weak smile didn't seem to be enough to reassure her. "It's nothing, just teenage hormones. I'll be okay in a minute."

"Crap," she said. "I thought fifteen was bad, if this is what eighteen looks like then I don't want any part of it."

I actually laughed a little. Leave it to Mattie to pull me out of it.

"You know if you ever need to talk to someone, I'm here. I can shut up long enough to be a good listener when I try," she said, looking way older than her tender years.

"Thanks," I said, splashing water on my face again and pulling some gum from my purse. I had to start doing better, I couldn't go through life like this. "Don't tell anybody about this, okay?" I said, she knew who I was talking about. Nodding her head, she gave me a reassuring hug.

.o0o.

I stepped into Mr. Thompson's class at the last moment. No way was I spending time discussing my crying jag with Scott James. Of course the only open seat was right next to him. He was still in silent treatment purgatory. Nobody would voluntarily sit next to the pariah. Nobody except me.

His eyebrows narrowed in concern as he flashed me a look of pure care. My heart melted into a gooey mess. You can do this, I mumbled to myself. Shake it off and pretend likes it's no big deal. I smiled at him, trying to reassure him that everything was great.

Mr. Thompson was handing out paper. The students started letting out groans as they read them. My stomach gave a lurch dreading what was coming.

"I've decided to pair you up for your semi-annual term paper," he said to the class before handing me a paper. There, third group down – Rivers/James --. Any other time I'd have been ecstatic to have been teamed with Scott, Heaven knew I could use the help and he was smarter than god when it came to History. I glanced at him from under my bangs and he smiled, obviously relieved also.

My heart smiled every time I looked at him. These people didn't deserve to be in the same room as him. Okay, I might have exaggerated a little. You know what I mean. I got mad every time I thought about what they were doing to him. His senior year was ruined because some bitch couldn't keep her pants on. I'd do anything to make it all go away for him.

## Chapter Eight
### Scott

New goal, make Katie happy. Make her senior year something to remember. I could do this, it didn't mean I was interested or anything. Even if she had that whole sexy librarian thing going for her. A guy could care about making her life interesting without being interested. Right?

Okay, I was interested as hell. I shouldn't have been. I knew this was the wrong time. Probably the wrong girl. All I knew was it was important to me that she smile. It made my day.

She was like a skittish colt. Too fast and she'd bolt. Or worse, dig herself into a hole so deep she'd never come out.

Katie left half way thru the game saying she had to help her aunt with something. She waved and caught Mattie's attention during a break then flashed a thumbs up and mimed she was leaving. Mattie nodded and waved good-bye.

After the game I headed out to warm up the truck while Mattie changed. I pulled my jacket in tight and stuck my hands in my pockets as I walked into the empty school parking lot. Who schedules a basketball game the day before Christmas break?

A light snow covered the ground, it'd please Grandfather. More snow now meant less water needed later. The soft breath of a breeze brought a faint wood smoke smell to the town. Winter had arrived.

"Hey Scott," Someone said behind me as I reached to open my door. My back tensed up, I knew that voice. Was it going to be now, the fight that I'd been anticipating and/or dreading for these last two months?

Danny stood there alone, his white cast pocking out from his jacket sleeve. He'd obviously waited for me to come out. My hands instinctively clinched into fists. I couldn't believe he had the guts to face me alone.

He smiled that silly smirk of his and shrugged his shoulders as if he'd swiped a French fry from my plate.

"What do you want," I asked.

He hesitated a moment and ran his hand through his hair. "For what it's worth, it wasn't about you," he said with a sheepish grin.

My blood boiled. It wasn't about me. I swear, did he think everything revolved around him. I unclenched my fists and let my shoulders slump. We wouldn't be fighting, not today. "What do want Danny, you can't fix this with a silly smile and wink."

He looked down and kicked a stone. At least he had the grace to look embarrassed. "Well, at least it didn't take you long to find someone new."

My forehead creased in confusion. What the hell was he talking about?

"That library girl," he said with frown. "I hear she's knocked up. The girls said she spends half the day throwing up in the bathroom." The straight lips and narrowed brow gave him a look of disgust that was unusual for him." Like mother, like daughter you know."

Katie? Did he mean Katie? I immediately dismissed the pregnancy rumor. No way was that true. Then it hit me, they thought we were together. What, did he think I could jump from girl to girl like him? He probably thought everyone was like him. Gina and he deserved each other. I turned to get into my truck. Mattie would be waiting and believe me, he wasn't worth my time.

"Scott," he said. "Be careful, she's not what you think."

What in the hell did he mean by that. The fact that he was talking about her made my skin crawl. He didn't deserve to be in the same world as her. "Listen Danny, You and your friends stay away from her. If you don't, that broken wrist will be the least of your problems. You got me?" I said, holding his gaze and burning the message into his soul.

Seeing that he got it, I jumped into the truck and spun out of there, making sure to spray enough gravel and dirt. Hopefully some of it would pop that silly smile of his.

.oOo.

<u>Katie</u>

Who would have believed that I'd miss school? Five days off and eleven to go and I was already bored out of my mind. It wasn't learning new wonderful things I missed. Lunch and sixth period more than anything. I'd spent a good deal of last night trying to figure out some way to call Scott. I almost called Mattie and hoped Scott answered. How pathetic is that.

Aunt Jenny mumbled to herself in the kitchen. Her head buried in a cupboard. "What are you doing Aunt Jenny," I asked.

"Looking for the vanilla."

"Why?"

"Christmas Cookies," she said pulling out of the cupboard with her prize and a large smile. When she smiled like that she reminded me of my mom. But mom never made Christmas cookies. "I'll take 'em around to some friends tomorrow."

"Wow, that sounds neat, can I help?" I'd never made Christmas cookies either. Maybe it was time I learned.

"Sure, we'll make double batches and you can give some to your friends."

She really had no clue, I didn't have friends. I thought about Mattie, and Scott, and even Kevin. They were friends. A person couldn't ask for better. "Could you take me out to the James's farm to drop off some cookies, I think it's out on highway Thirty Three." My heart stopped while waiting for an answer. She nodded and said it'd be no problem. My heart started again and my palms began to sweat.

We spent the day buried in flour and up to our elbows in chocolate chips and sugar icing. I couldn't remember when I had a better time with an adult. Aunt Jenny was pretty cool when you thought about it. She had a messed up teenager dumped on her door and she hadn't batted an eye. Hadn't pressed me for details. Hadn't laid down the law. She only had a couple of rules. Keep my room clean, and let her know where I was at. Help with the house work and pick-up after myself.

After a while the whole house wore that delicious fresh cookie smell that made your tummy rumble and nose surrender. I learned how to decorate cookies with cake icing. Making pretty Christmas shapes in red and green.

After the last batch, she sighed then pulled an index card out of the back of her recipe box.

"What's that?" I asked.

She looked hesitatingly at it then back at me. "It's my mom's, Your Grandmother's recipe for divinity. Last year was the first Christmas I didn't have any." She shook her head. "Your grandmother's divinity was famous throughout half the county."

My lungs felt like they were empty and I swear I almost cried right there in the kitchen over a desert confection. "Are we going to make some?" I asked.

She thought for a moment and said, "Yes we are. Especially if you're taking it out to the James' place. Scotty James always did love my mother's divinity."

It took me a second to realize she was talking about Scott's grandfather. We finished the cookies and then made my grandmothers divinity. When we were done I made sure to copy the recipe into my journal.

The next morning dragged by as I took a little extra time getting ready. I'd called Mattie to ask if they were home. She'd laughed and said where else would they be. I could tell the off days were getting to her too.

My wardrobe was seriously lacking. I'd spent the morning going through everything I owned and came up way short. What did a person wear to deliver Christmas cookies?

I settled on my favorite, okay tightest, Jeans and a fitted green shirt. It matched my eyes. And I've got to admit, highlighted my shape very well.

This is no big deal, you're just going to deliver some cookies for gosh sake. I kept telling myself. It didn't matter how often I said it, my heart continued to race and my palms continued to sweat.

I came out of my room to find Aunt Jenny standing there with an unwrapped box. "I planned on giving you this for Christmas. Something tells me you could use it now." She held out the box with smiling eyes. I could tell she was as excited about this present as I was.

Taking the heavy box to the dining table, I lifted the lid. I'll admit that I squealed. My aunt had given me the most beautiful calf length wool grey pea coat with wooden toggle and rope buttons. I held it at arm's length and marveled at how beautiful it was.

I put it on and ran to the bathroom to see what it looked like. It fit perfectly. A woman's coat. Aunt Jenny smiled and held out a matching set of gloves, wool knit cap, and white scarf. I couldn't believe it. Wait until Scott saw me in this.

We gathered our cookie filled platters. I floated out the door and into Aunt Jenny's Mazda. We were five minutes into the trip when I asked Aunt Jenny about my mom and whether she'd liked making Christmas cookies. My aunt laughed and shook her head.

"Your mom hated the kitchen. She'd rather vacuum the whole house than make a sandwich."

"What was she like, growing up I mean." I couldn't believe I asked. We never talked about the past. The first six months with her I'd sort of been in a daze the whole time. It sort of became habit. An unspoken rule, neither of us delved too deep into the past.

Aunt Jenny thought for a moment and seemed to make up her mind.

"Wild from the day they brought her home from the hospital." A secret smile crossed her lips with a fond memory. "Always pushing the boundaries. I was the older sister. I was the one who was supposed to break the rules first. Your mom beat me to every single one."

I looked at her, she was still attractive. I felt brave so asked, "Why didn't you ever get married Aunt Jenny. I mean, you're a pretty woman, you know how to make killer Christmas cookies. What more could a guy ask for.

She laughed, but didn't answer my question right away. Finally she said, "I guess because I let the right one get away." After a long pause she continued. "In my junior year I had a massive crush on a senior. We dated for a time. It was wonderful. But my dad was never happy about it."

She sighed again "I gave this boy a hard time about leaving me and going to college. We broke up. It was mostly my idea. I think I wanted to break up before he left. It sort of made me think I was in control. He came back four years later with a wife and a two year old son." Her eyes clouded over into a lost world for a moment then she chuckled and shrugged her shoulders.

I wondered about what she'd said. "What happened with my mom, why'd she leave town."

"Dad and she fought like cats and dogs. He was the pastor and said we had to set an example. She used to say it was none of his business and run around. There wasn't anything he could do. I didn't know why she left until you showed up. Not long after turning sixteen she disappeared. She left a note, but it didn't really explain. We never heard another word until I got the call from the social worker in California."

It was hard to believe that mom was two years younger than me when she left. I wondered what her life had been like. Slowly I realized that she'd been pregnant with me when she left. Did anyone here in town know what had happened? Maybe my father was from this town. Had gone to the same school I was going to. Had I met him and not known? Was it possible to meet your father and not know it was him? Wouldn't I be able to recognize him? My heart pounded as my mind began to fly to all of the questions and issues surrounding my unknown dad.

The car fell into a heavy silence for the rest of the trip until Aunt Jenny slowed down to pull onto the James' road. You couldn't call it a driveway, at almost a quarter mile it passed between snow-covered fields with corn stalk stubble poking through.

My heart was pounding a thousand times a minute as we pulled into the dirt yard behind the idyllic farm house. The place looked like a Currier and Ives poster, midwest edition. A light green old house made of wooden clapboards. With a porch extending all the way around. Smoke rose from a field stone chimney making the place look inviting and more than willing to welcome you. My palms continued to sweat, I couldn't believe how nervous I was.

The yard was laid out in an irregular triangle shape with a gray metal garage on one side and a fire engine red Dutch barn on the other. Before we came to a stop Mattie stormed out of the house letting the screen door bang behind her. She wore a flowery print apron and was busy drying her hands as she walked towards us.

A black and white border collie rushed from the barn, barking once before sidling up to Mattie as if protecting her from these evil non-pack members. Mattie was so lucky to have a dog.

The earthy smell of manure and old hay struck me as I stepped out of the car. I quickly scanned the yard. No Scott. Was he here? I hadn't asked Mattie if he'd be there when I called her. I didn't want to be too obvious. My heart dropped at the thought that I might not get to see him today.

You've got it bad Kate, I thought.

On older man came out of the house, and used the rail to come down the stairs one step at a time. This must be their grandfather. I could see Scott in his eyes and his wide shoulders but he had Mattie's lips and forehead.

"You're here," Mattie said rushing up and giving me a quick hug. She stepped back, dropped her hands and looked at my new coat. "Wow, I like it. You look great," she said forcing me to twirl so she could see it all.

"Hi Miss Rivers," she said to my aunt, "Thanks you for bringing Katie all the way out here." My aunt nodded and returned her smile.

"Hello Jennifer, it's nice to see you again," Mr. James said walking up and shaking my aunt's hand. She looked into his face tentatively then reached out and gave him a big hug.

"Yes, it has been a while hasn't it,"

Mr. James was obviously taken aback by the hug then relaxed and returned it with full force. "Won't you come in, both of you. Mattie just put a pot of coffee on."

"Oh, I forgot," I said, as I dove back into the car and retrieved the platter of cookies. I held it out for Mattie and said, "Merry Christmas."

"We included some of my mother's Divinity," Aunt Jenny said to Mr. James. His face lit up and he rushed around the front of the car at least as fast as his old legs would let him. A large smile lit up his face as he took the platter from Mattie.

"You remembered, thank you," He said with a smile from ear to ear.

"Actually, Katie did most of the work," Aunt Jenny said. Now that wasn't close to being true. Why was my aunt trying to build me up in their grandfather's eyes? Believe me, I didn't mind. It just wasn't something I was used to. And where was Scott? I was dying to ask. It took every bit of will power and strength not to blurt out the question.

Mattie grabbed my elbow and started to pull me towards the house. Aunt Jenny saw and said, "Actually we can't stay, I've got a lot more deliveries, we really must be going." Mattie's lips turned down in a little girl pout. She didn't say anything. Her eyes begging me to fix this.

My heart slid to a halt, I wasn't going to see Scott. I wanted to see his face when he saw our cookies. I wanted him to see me in my new coat. I wanted to see him.

# Certain Rules

Period. At that moment, the object of my fantasies walked out of the metal garage like a knight walking across a battle field.

He wore a red plaid flannel shirt with the sleeve rolled up exposing hard tanned forearms. His hands were covered in black oil as he wiped them on a filthy rag. I wanted to hand him a box of my handy wipes. A short streak of black oil smeared his forehead. I smiled at the thought of him wiping his hair out of his eyes.

His deep dark eyes struck me like a physical blow. They bore into me, cataloging every detail. As if he'd never seen me before. Scanning my body, making it tingle all over. Our eyes met and I couldn't tare myself away. It was as if we were falling together into a deep pool with no bottom.

A gentle cough behind me helped me pull out. I turned to see my Aunt trying to hide a smile. "Actually, Katie can stay for a little bit and I can stop by and pick her up later. If that's all right with you Mr. James?"

Mattie jumped in before her grandfather could answer. "That's great, she could stay for dinner and Scott could take her home. That be okay with you," she asked me. Her face already scheming.

Glancing at Scott to see if he was okay with this, I caught him staring at me again. The tingle throughout my body was becoming a regular thing and could easily become addicting. He smiled and nodded his head without taking his eyes off of me.

## Chapter Nine
### Scott

As long as I live, I will never forget seeing her standing there in my yard looking like a model out of one those fashion magazines. Her cute white scarf thrown over her shoulder.

My heart stopped and I became very aware of my filthy hands. Mattie hadn't told me that Katie would be dropping by. A matter I'd deal with later.

Her Aunt left with a wave and Grandfather carried the plate of cookies into the house. Mattie looked back and forth between Katie and I then shook her head and mumbled something about having to take care of something in the kitchen before leaving us.

The world narrowed and everything not Katie dropped away. We continued to stare at each other for a moment, neither of us talking. She started to blush and broke the glance to stare at her feet. I finally remembered my manners and escorted into the house.

I helped her out of her coat and hung it by the door. I think we'd have fallen into another staring contest if Grandfather hadn't stepped in carrying a chess board. We played a game most afternoons during the winter when the work load wasn't so oppressive. Couldn't he realize that chess was the last thing I wanted to do this afternoon?

"Come on, I'll give you the grand tour," Mattie said, leading her up the stairs. I quickly gave a silent prayer that I'd cleaned my room. Oh okay, semi cleaned up. The laundry pile was smaller than normal and I'd put away the clean clothes.

"This is my room," Mattie said from the top of the stairs throwing open her door. Her room was spotless I'm sure, as always. Decorated in typical girly fashion stuffed animals on the bed and posters of Rodeo Champion Eric Tomas on the wall.

Grandfather and I were playing chess at the kitchen table when the girls walked in. "I've got winners," Mattie said as she checked the roast in the oven. The savory aroma of roasting meat washed throughout the entire house making my spit glands work overtime.

We'd spent countless evenings at this very table while my grandmother had prepared dinner. She liked to have us around so she could needle Grandfather or impulsively hug Mattie or me.

My mind wandered and I found myself staring at Katie. I honestly think that she had no idea how pretty she was. Full red lips, sparkling white teeth. I wanted to run my hands over her skin, it looked so smooth and soft. It felt strange seeing her in these cloths, good strange. They emphasized her long curving torso, I couldn't stop myself from sneaking looks.

The chess game had lost all ability to hold my interest. I moved my rook, Grandfather grumbled and shot me a look of confusion. Then took my queen.

"Dinner smells wonderful," Katie said. "Can I help?"

"No thank you, it's pretty much done, were just waiting for the meat to finish up," Mattie answered.

"Where did you learn to cook Mattie?" Katie asked.

"My Ellen taught her," Grandfather said, getting a faraway look when he said her name.

"Yeah, she said I had to take care of these two," Mattie said indicating Grandfather and I. "She said I had to take care of them until I was eighteen. And that I wasn't to take care of them after that. She figured they'd be old enough to take care of themselves by then."

Katie chuckled and sat next to me to watch the game. My pulse immediately jumped into warp drive as the air between us began to tingle and sparkle. A long uncomfortable silence descended until Mattie joined us and kept a conversation going with occasional input from the rest of us.

Grandfather put me in check mate and shook his head. "That has to be the worst game you've played in years. What's going on?"

I glanced at Katie and felt my face flush, I'm sure she'd picked up on what was going on. Turning to Mattie she asked about Chrissy, her horse. I appreciated the effort to deflect the attention away from me.

"I'm worried about her, she's due to foal next week."

"Do you want to go see her," I asked, jumping at a chance to get out of the house and away from Grandfathers discerning eye.

"Sure, that'd be great," Katie said, her eyes lighting up with excitement.

As she reached for her coat I put a hand out and shook my head. "You don't want to wear that into the barn, Here, use this," I said holding out my red and white letterman's jacket. Her eyes grew as large as pumpkins and her faced turned a delicious shade of pink. She slipped her arm into it and was immediately swallowed up. Pulling the sleeves up she hugged it close and followed me out to the barn.

The jacket fell half way to her thighs and made her sexy as hell. The girl could wear anything and look great. Seeing her in my jacket sent a special thrill down my spine.

.oOo.

Katie

Katie Rivers was wearing Scott James Letterman Jacket, who would ever have believed it. I pulled it in close and buried my nose on the inside. Scott's musky aftershave washed through me and lit me on fire. Careful Katie, I said to myself. He's being nice, remember he's in love with Gina Woods – That B...

Scott held the barn door open for me and gave me his patented flourish to usher me in. I chuckled to myself and stepped in to be hit by a wave of smells. Manure, animal hair, and old wood all combined to let me know exactly where I was and how different this was from the suburbs of southern California.

Jack, their black and white collie came to greet us, his fluffy tail whipping back and forth in excitement. He stuck his nose into Scott's hand then scrunched down as Scott scratched his back.

A cow in the first stall mooed making me jump and bump into Scott. He reached out to catch me. I felt his fingers grip my shoulder and didn't flinch. I softened into his hold and had to check myself from leaning into him. "What's her name?" I asked.

"It's a him and he doesn't have a name. We don't normally name them if we're going to eat them."

I blanched and felt like a fool. Of course they don't name them. You idiot, this is a different world Katie. The next stall held a medium sized pig, obviously future bacon. As we made our way down the central aisle chickens scratched in the dirt and hay before scattering out of our way. Scott pointed out the coop covered in wire fencing. A white hen sat on a nest in a wooden box, A dozen little yellow chicks dancing around her.

The thought that they were future food dampened the mood a little. My mind instantly switched mode when Scott held my hand and gently pulled me towards the last stall. A wooden sign with the word Chrissy painted in pink adorned the wall next to the half Dutch door. A bucket of horse tools, combs and brushes sat under the sign ready for use.

When I peaked inside, a beautiful chestnut brown and very pregnant horse looked back at me with huge chocolate eyes covered in thick lashes. She stood in the center of the stall and looked at us with the saddest expression.

Scott muttered under his breath and slowly opened the door. He stepped in first and motioned me inside. He nodded towards the wall and said, "Hold on a second while I check her out. She doesn't look right. She should have come to meet us at the door."

I nodded that I understood and backed up to lean against the wall while he slowly walked towards the horse. He reached into his pocket and retrieved a raw carrot with the green top attached. He held it out for her and started to gently rub her neck while whispering. "How you doing girl." He continued on down. Running his hand across her giant belly before making his way to the back where he lifted her tail and shook his head at what he saw. As he examined her a gush of fluid shot out and drenched him from collar to belt.

I squealed then started to laugh so hard I thought for sure I'd pee my pants. He looked so shocked. His brow scowled and face scrunched up. He obviously didn't enjoy being laughed at. I clamped down on my giggles but I couldn't stop smiling.

Chrissy looked back at him but didn't move. Letting out a big sigh she settled to her knees before slowly rolling onto her side. My heart jumped into my throat with worry. Was she sick? "What's going on, is she okay?" I asked.

"Her water broke, Can you go get Mattie for me. Tell her that Chrissy has started her delivery. And ask her to bring me a new shirt. Thanks," he said reaching back and pulling his shirt off. He used the dry side to wipe his face. I was transfixed. He was so big. Everything was in perfect proportions, just more of it than should be allowed. His wide shoulders and arms were as hard as granite. His barrel chest looked like a solid wall of stone tapering down to a hard stomach. A fine dusting of chest hair narrowed to a point aimed at his belt buckle and what lay beneath his pants. My heart race and I licked my lips, trying to swallow had become impossible.

He looked up and caught me staring. My face grew warm. I couldn't look away. He coughed and brought me back to reality. I hurried out the door and into the house.

Mattie squealed when I told her. She asked her grandfather to finish dinner and ran upstairs to get Scott a shirt.

We were back in Chrissy's stall within minutes. Mattie immediately dropped to her knees next to the horses head and started stroking her cheek. She glanced up at my terrified face and smiled. "Don't worry. Scott's the best when it comes to horses, he'll take care of her."

Scott pulled on the new shirt and I felt a brief sense of regret. He smirked and shrugged his shoulders. "It looks like a normal delivery, no need to call the vet."

Not call the vet? How could they not call the vet? This horse was everything to Mattie. They couldn't risk her. How dare they not call the animal doctor? My ire started to come up before I reminded myself this wasn't my world. Don't try and tell the experts what they should do. Still, I worried they were wrong.

He finished tucking his shirt into his pants them stepped out. He came bac carrying a sixty pound bale of hay like it he held a pack of marshmallows. He placed it next to the wall out of the way. "Have a seat it's going to be a bit," he said to me then returned to the horse to examiner her again.

We must have been there a couple of hours when their grandfather popped his head over the Dutch door and said, "How's she doing"

"Shouldn't be much longer, Hour, hour and half," Scott said.

"Well, I brought you all dinner, no use letting it go to waste." He said handing out sandwiches. The delicious aroma of roast beef and fresh bread made my mouth water. My stomach rumbled in anticipation. I looked over at Mr. James in surprise. He saw my raised eyebrows and smiled. "Don't look so surprised, I can make a sandwich. I did learn a few things over the years."

Scott washed his hands in a bucket of water then sat next to me on the hay bail. Our legs rubbed against each other sending warm shock waves up and down my leg. I didn't move away but focused on my dinner. I thought about the school cafeteria. It was amazing how far from school this was. No wonder he could stay so grounded. There were so many things more important than the social scene at a small high school.

We finished our wonderful dinner in silence. My face grew warm and probably a little pink when I thought about what Scott must think seeing me scarf down that sandwich. He knocked my shoulder with his and smiled as he finished his dinner.

"Your Grandfather must trust you a lot to leave you to do this by yourself," I said.

Scott's eyebrows narrowed in confusion for a moment as he shrugged his shoulders. "I guess. I never thought about it that way." He shook his head as he pondered the situation then settled back into a comfortable silence as we waited.

Sitting on that bale of hay was one of the most fun things I have ever done. My pulse raced as if I were riding a roller coaster, a big one. Every sense had come to full alert. The other animals sounded as clear as if I was in the stall with them. Mattie's whispers were clear and soothing.

The smells of the barn burnt the back of my throat, leaving a rich, deep taste. Scott had that horsey scent that reminded me of nature and that I'd always associate with this day. The barn smell became softer and more natural the longer I sat there.

The hay prickled the backs of my legs but felt solid and comforting. It was impossible to ignore the man sitting next to me. The heat Scott generated seeped into my bones as I snuggled into his jacket. Bliss. I was worried about Mattie's horse, but I wasn't worried about me. How long had it been since I felt that?

"This might be a while; you should probably call your Aunt and let her know you'll be a little late. I don't want to leave until it's over"

Wow, extra innings I thought and smiled inside. I could sit there next to him all night.

"Scott!" Mattie hissed as the big brown horse started to try and get up. Finally she got her right front leg under her, then the left. Snorting she slowly stood with a heavy horsey groan. I caught a glimpse of her back end, things were red and disgusting. My stomach rolled over and I thought I'd puke right there in front of everybody. But stood and forced it back down.

Scott walked back to the horse and gently rubbed her backbone before moving to check how she was doing. "Don't worry about calling your aunt."

I swallowed hard but couldn't look away. A red and grey gooey mess started to emerge from the horse. It looked like the alien from the movies that tore its way out of people's chest. Chrissy gave a push but nothing more happened. Was it stuck? See I knew they should have gotten a vet. What if she needed a cesarean?

Scott held her tail out of the way as reached up and gently stuck his finger into the horse. "Easy Girl," he muttered in a quiet voice, his brow creased in concentration. A moment later a black hoof popped free. Chrissy pushed and a long gray gooey mess started to emerge. I couldn't believe this. I was watching a horse get born.

A small horse head and two perfect little feet showed themselves. My heart raced as I couldn't look away. Suddenly without warning Chrissy grunted and my heart skipped as the grey and red form rushed from her and into Scott's arms.

He caught the foal and eased it to the ground. Mattie griped the halter and continued to whisper sweet words into Chrissy's ear. Her eyes continually darting back toward Scott trying to see what was going on.

Scott ran his finger through the foal's mouth then gathered a hand full of clean straw from the stall floor and wiped the little foal. He gently massaged the animal's muscles, helping him to start breathing and begin his new life. My heart melted into a puddle watching him.

Mattie kissed Chrissy on the nose then let go of her halter so she could check out her new baby. Mattie walked over to stand next to me. Scott joined us. A strong whiff of blood and afterbirth overwhelmed the barn manure smell. His face and shirt were covered in horse fluids.

My heart turned over every time I thought about it. To see innocent life introduced into the world sent a firm bolt of electricity right through me. I could tell that both Mattie and Scott were as impressed as me. I felt privileged and so thankful.

The brand new foal was all knobby knees and huge chocolate eyes. A blaze of white like a Christmas star covered its forehead and matched the four white stockings. I wanted to throw my arms around it and hug his neck for the next week.

"Is it a boy or girl?" I asked

"It's a colt," Scott said. "A boy," he added because of my confused look.

"What are you going to name him," I asked Mattie.

She shrugged her shoulders and said, "I think it's going to have to be Star." We chuckled because she was right. No other name would do.

Star wobbled to his knees then to his shaky feet. He swayed back and forth as if he might fall over. My heart went out to him, I wanted to walk over and help keep him steady. Chrissy didn't seem too concerned as she waited for him to get stable.

He took a few hesitant steps finally grasped the concept and began to move more easily. He hurriedly made his way to his mother's belly where he started pushing with his nose trying to find his first dinner. All three of us laughed at his antics.

After a few minutes Scott said, "Let's give them some peace. Mattie will check on them throughout the night. I can take you home, if you're ready?"

My heart stopped and my stomach dropped. I didn't want to leave. Everything was so wonderful here, full of life and the drama was important not silly, useless things.

Nodding my head I started to follow him out of the stall but turned and went back to give Chrissy a goodbye pat on her neck. I leaned in and whispered my thanks for letting me be there to share this wonder event. I think she understood because she looked into my eyes and winked as if to say the world's a special place.

A huge silver moon bathed the yard in bright light. The air outside had that crisp burning wood smell and nipped at my loose hair and warm cheek.

"Mattie will kill me if I go inside with this messy shirt. Let me grab a shower then I'll take you home," he said as he pulled his shirt off for the second time that night.

Yes most definitely, the world was a special place.

## Chapter Ten
### Scott

Katie couldn't stop smiling as I held the truck door open for her. She hopped in and buckled up as I made my way around the vehicle. This was going to be an interesting ride home, I thought. It would be the first time we were truly alone together. Just the two of us.

God she looked good. The dashboard lights bathed her in a soft glow. Highlighting her gorgeous face and sending shivers up and down my spine. Those glasses and the form fitting coat that hugged her shape. Plus she'd put her hair into a high pony tail. It gave her a sexy prim look that tickled my insides to a flutter. Squeezing my heart a little.

She'd pushed a wisp of her lustrous auburn hair behind her ears and flashed me a smile that thrust clear through my heart. What was it about this girl?

My gut tightened into a hard knot whenever I thought about her. It freaked me out a little to think about getting involved with someone again. There was no way I was going through that again. Gina had taught me a lesson I wouldn't soon forget.

My knuckles turned white on the steering wheel as I tried to regain control of my emotions. She's not like Gina I told myself in the understatement of the year. Katie's soft and warm and an old fashioned sweet. It's important to her that those she cares about are happy. It's a different perspective. Gina wanted those around her to make her happy.

It was like a nuclear explosion went off in my head when I realized the difference and all the signs that pointed to it. We always had to do what Gina wanted or her lips would curl into a frown and pout like a little girl. Danny, you pour slob, I thought and chuckled.

"What?" Katie asked, as her eyebrows rose in question.

"Nothing really," I said. "So tell me, why'd you move in with your aunt? Southern California so boring you had to come to our giant metropolis in the heartland of Nebraska to finding any action?"

The smile dropped from her face and she scrunched into the corner like a trapped rabbit facing a hungry mountain lion. My heart stopped and adrenalin pumped through my muscles. What had I done? "Jesus Katie, I'm sorry. It was just an innocent question. You can tell me to mind my own business, or better yet. To shut up and leave you alone."

She relaxed a little and gently shook her head. She stared off through the window at the black night for a movement. "My mom's in jail, prison," she said. It was like someone had let the air out of a balloon as she shrunk in on herself and hunched up waiting for an explosion.

Wow, I hadn't expected that. My heart went out to her, she looked so lost, so hurt. My god what had that been like, especially for a girl like Katie. I could just imagine how her friends had acted. She'd been through all that and still voluntarily helped me.

"Prison? Did she hurt you?" I asked as I held my breath waiting for an answer. My heart turned over at the thought of anyone ever hurting this girl.

"She's doing two to five years for prostitution." Katie continued. That scared rabbit look was back as she watched me and waited for my reaction.

I shook my head in shock then furrowed my brow in confusion. Prostitution? That seemed a long time, but what do I know. Katie saw may confusion and said, "Yeah, I know, it is a long time. That's what they do when you get arrested six times and convicted for the third."

"Wow, are you okay, I can imagine that was all pretty hard on you."

She let out a long sigh then looked at me with tears in her eyes. They sat on the edge ready to spill at the slightest disturbance. She nodded and said, "Yeah, I'm fine, it's all behind me now." Her eyes looked up to the truck roof. And I knew she was lying. It had to have been the first time she'd ever lied to me.

Jack's convenience store was coming up and I pulled into the parking lot. Parked and turned the engine off before putting my arm over the back of the bench seat and turning to look at her. Her eyebrows had risen half way up her forehead as she questioned what I was doing.

"I didn't want to get in a wreck, besides. I can't take you home like this. Your aunt will think I tried something."

She laughed "Yeah, like you'd ever try anything. I'd kick your butt and you know it." She got all serious on me again like turning a light switch. "You're the first person I've ever told. My Aunt Jenny knows because the social worker told her. She's never questioned me about it, she let me know the first night she was available if I wanted to talk. But it wasn't something I could ever bring up. I was way too embarrassed."

That wasn't all of it, something happened to her somewhere along the way, something real bad. She turned away from me to watch a young family leave the dinner. The man was dressed in jeans and a button down shirt with a suede leather coat. The woman wore a dress and puffy parka. Each of them held the hand of a little girl in pig tails. I don't know why I was paying attention to them except they'd captured Katie's fascination. She stared and started talking. It was like somebody had opened a hose as it all rushed from her.

"It was never something I knew about growing up. I was twelve before I realized what was going on. I thought everybody's mom would get calls in the middle of the night and take off for a couple of hours. When I was little she'd leave me with Mrs. Alverez. By the time I was about eight, Mrs. Alverez moved back to Mexico and Mom just left me alone. The times Mom was gone for more than a day or two I'd hang out at Mrs. Caluchi's house. Social services never knew I existed. Mrs. Alverez was illegal, no way was she calling the government. Mrs. Caluchi hated the government and wouldn't have called them if her house was on fire."

My heart squeezed shut thinking about a little girl growing up in that kind of home. I used to think I had it bad with Grandfather. I had to give him credit. He was always there when we needed him. We never had to worry about who would take care of us.

"The last time, some things happened," She said. She shuddered as if a ghost had walked across her grave. She shook it off and continued. "Anyway, the authorities learned about my existence and tracked down Aunt Jenny. I didn't even know I had an aunt."

"What about your dad?" I asked.

She gave me that familiar lost patient from the asylum look and snorted. "I never knew my dad. Until today I figured he was some john with a broken condom."

"What happened today?" I asked and twisted in my seat. This was getting interesting.

"On the way to your guy's house my Aunt Jenny mentioned something that made me realize my mom was probably pregnant with me before she left town. She was only sixteen." Katie lifter her hand to her mouth and gasped. "My god, she was a year older than Mattie. Two years younger than me."

The mention of Mattie and her mother's situation in the same sentence made my stomach clench up into a knot. Raising a kid on your own had to be tough. Doing it without social services or welfare had to have been hell on both the mom and the kid.

"I can't believe I am telling you all of this," she said.

"You know Katie I like listening. That way I don't have to do the talking. Besides, if you ever need it, I have big shoulders

.o0o.

Katie

Scott seemed to be taking it pretty well. I couldn't read him but he wasn't throwing me out of the truck so it was something. There is an unspoken rule for kids. Your parents should be respectable. Even when teenagers bitch and complain about how bad their parents are and how they'll never be like that when they have kids. Still, deep down, it is important their parents be respectable, that they not bring shame on the family. That's the kid's job.

My hands were clasped together in my lap like eagle talons. My hair had fallen in front of my face but I couldn't let go long enough to push it out of the way. The handy wipe packet in my front pocket was burning a hole into my leg, demanding to get out and clean away the shame. But still I couldn't move.

"I've got a couple of questions," Scott said.

My heart jumped into my throat, here it comes. "Okay," I whispered.

"What's your middle name," he said like he was asking the time of day. "Mine's O'Brian, not Brian, but O'Brian. It was my mom's maiden name. It always gets screwed up on the school district paperwork. Someone thinks I don't know my own middle name and changes it. I sort of like it though. Different you know."

My eyes bugged out, what did that have to do with what I'd been talking about? Did he hear what I said?

"I already know your favorite desert is cheesecake," he said with a smile.

My brain was floundering around trying to figure out what was going on. I gave up and answered, "Sharri, Katherine Sharri Rivers. No reason, just a name." I said trying not to look at him like he had three heads.

He nodded, accepting my answer. "What's your favorite color," he continued as if we were passing the time of day. He stayed twisted towards me with his arm along the back rest. His eyes bore into me with curiosity. "No let me guess, green, forest green in fact."

"Yes, how'd you know," I asked, more amazed that he'd noticed than how this conversation was going.

"Oh your eyes are a green that reminds me of spring corn. And you wear a lot of green, it goes good with your hair. Okay, now tell me what your last school was like?"

What could I tell him, that my last school was boring? Filled with people I didn't know. How life was about keeping my distance. Not letting anyone know anything about me and my family. Maybe I should tell him how my stomach was in a permanent knot. Fearing what would happen when everyone found out what my mother was. I know, I could tell him that my biggest fear is some strange boy walking up to me in front of everyone waiving a bunch of twenties in my face and asking me to have sex for a hundred dollars.

Instead I looked at him and shrugged my shoulders. "It was your typical school, nothing special," I said. I knew it wasn't going to be enough when I said it.

"Come on, you can do better than that. Was it fully of Barbie types and surfer dudes?"

I laughed, "There were a few."

"What were your school's dances like? Full blown formal affairs, like the prom every month. Or kicked back and informal, cutoffs and flip flops," he said, his lips curled up in a smile.

My shoulders relaxed a fraction and I shook the hair out of my face and shrugged my shoulders again. "I don't know. I never went to any of the dances."

"You didn't," he said, his eyes opening wide. "I know you haven't gone to any of them here. I would have noticed. Are you telling me you've never been to a high school dance?"

My face grew warm and I shook my head no. What was so special about high school dances anyway?

"Hmm, interesting, well in that case. Would you like to go with me to the dance in a couple of weeks? Everyone should go to at least one high school dance in their life. If anything, so they can see how awful they are and look back on them in happiness that they never have to do it again."

"Wow, you make it sound so romantic."

"Hey, I think I'm doing pretty good here. Don't ruin the moment." He said with a chuckle. Fear flashed through me, did he think I was easy. Was that why he asked me out. I suddenly realized that I was alone with him in a deserted parking lot. My heart raced for a moment.

I looked at him again and knew that wasn't what was going on. Scott wouldn't treat a person that way. My heart melted right there and then. This boy had turned one of my most embarrassing and heart wrenching moments into a joyful memory. I knew that for as long as I lived I'd always treasure this conversation with him. For the first time there was a corner I could turn, an opportunity to start looking at life a little differently.

I smiled back at him. His forehead was creased and his eyes were focused on mine. I realized he was nervous waiting for an answer. What must it have taken for him to put himself out there again? Especially so soon after being crushed by Gina.

Nodding my head I said "Yes, I would like to go to the dance with you." I immediately locked my eyes on the hands in my lap. Had I really just been asked out by Scott James, and said yes. My melted heart began to knit itself back together and I smiled to myself.

He started humming to himself - It sounded like "Singing in the Rain."- He twisted back around and started the truck.

.oOo.

We pulled into Aunt Jenny's drive way, the truck felt so warm and toasty that I never wanted to leave. He turned the truck off and held out a hand to stop me opening my door. "Let me," He said as he jumped out and ran around the front of the truck and opened my door holding out his hand to help me down. Obviously I didn't need any help but I placed my hand in his and let him. An electric shock traveled up my arm at the speed of light and shot strait into my soul. My cheeks were starting to hurt I was smiling so much. He must think I'm some kind of freak.

He held my hand as we continued to the door. I wondered if he would try to kiss me. God, what if he did and I freaked. Was I about to ruin this wonderful day. I stilled my heart and prepared myself. I could do this, I wanted to do this.

He looked down and stepped next to me. He was so tall I really had to crane my neck back. His chocolate eyes pulled me in and I felt myself floating.

"Thanks for the Christmas cookies," his deep voice soothed my ruffled edges.

It took me a moment to realize what he was talking about. It was all so long ago. I swallowed and nodded a "you're welcome." I couldn't seem to make my lips work enough to speak.

He continued to smile, started to lean forward. I felt it. Knew what was coming but he changed his mind and pulled back. "Goodnight Katharine," he said with a sad smile then turned and walked back to his truck. I felt a hollowness surround me as he left. That old familiar loneliness crept back in. I sighed and stepped inside praying I could avoid Aunt Jenny long enough to get my tumbled thoughts together. Wow what a day, I delivered Christmas cookies to my friends, watched a horse get born, told Scott one of my deepest secrets and not only didn't he run away screaming in the night, he asked me out to a dance. Okay, it was officially one of the greatest days of my life.

My phone beeped in my pocket. I pulled it out and switched to the text screen. "Sweet dreams Katie, It was a great day."

My heart melted once again, it was getting to be a habit. Oh boy Katie girl, you've got it bad. I smiled to myself and floated to my room.

## Chapter Eleven
### Scott

'Singing in the rain'? You've got to be kidding me. Where did that come from? I asked myself as I made my way home in a haze. Why did you ask her out, what were you thinking? I hadn't planned it, it bubbled up and burst out like a dam releasing overflow.

Jesus what a screwed up life she had. It sucked and made me feel all sick inside every time I thought about her having to go through it. I will never forget what her face had looked like when she told me about her mother. The fear and shame had been etched deep into her furrowed brow.

The porch light cast a yellow glow over the yard as I pulled in. I turned the truck off and slowly pounded my head into the steering wheel. What had I done and why? This was a road I hadn't planned on taking and didn't know for sure where it went. This girl's got more baggage than an airport carrousel, I thought. However, admit it Scott, you can't stop smiling. I was looking forward to the dance. I was looking forward to spending more time with Katie.

Jumping out of the truck I made my way to the barn to check on Chrissy and her foal before heading in for the night. Grandfather leaned on the stall's Dutch door watching the horses. He glanced up when I stepped into the barn and asked, "You get that girl home safe."

"Yes Sir," I answered.

He nodded his head and returned to watching the little colt. He appeared to be lost in thought. I couldn't really blame him as I leaned against the door and watched the foal scamper around the stall. Chrissy took it all in stride and would occasionally nudge him with her nose and get him into the right position to feed.

"I liked that girl, Katie, she reminded me of your mom."

Wow where did that come from? Grandfather was not known for offering unsolicited compliments about people.

"I didn't know you knew Katie's aunt," I said.

"Who, Jenny Rivers. I've known her since she was a little girl. She and your dad dated for a while in High school. In fact there was a time I thought they might end up married, but then you dad went off to college and came back with your mom."

Wow! Where did that come from?

"Don't look so surprised," he continued. "Things did exist before you were born you know."

I pondered what he said for a moment. The fact that my dad had a life before he met my mom was obvious, I'd never really thought about it. I'd grown up on stories about College, about the day he met my mom, stuff like that. But he'd gone to the same school as Mattie and I were attending. He had known the adults I knew, but he'd known them as kids and teenagers.

"Did you know Katie's mom?" I asked. Of course it was the subject of her father I wanted to talk about, but Grandfather is a little old fashioned. He wouldn't say anything bad about a woman's moral lapses. One of Grandfather's golden rules was that a girl shouldn't get pregnant at sixteen and shame on the boy that got her that way. I wondered what he'd think about a woman in jail for prostitution.

"Yeah I knew Margret Rivers, but mostly as Jenny's kid sister. She tagged alone on some of their adventures. They all hung out together, Stephan Carlson, Tommy Miller, The Carrs Brothers. As the boys got older, girls started to be included in the group. Jenny Rivers was one of them. Probably drove her father crazy. Their mother was an angel and made the best divinity in the county. Their father was a bit of prick though. Preachers can get that way. Had his nose so far in the air he would have drowned in a summer rain."

That summed it up in grandfather's mind. Everyone categorized and placed in their holder. And I knew the conversation was over. He'd already talked more than normal. If I pushed it he'd shut down and get all prickly. He hated talking about things from before. He always said the past wasn't important, let it go.

Star left his mother and wobbled to the two of us. Grandfather stretched and ruffled the foal's mane. Lost in thought. I wondered what he was thinking. He'd lost his only son, his wife who he adored, and his big powerful body was beginning to betray him. I swear to god a tear did not form in my eye, it was a piece of dust. I turned and wiped it away.

.oOo.

<u>Katie</u>

The first day back after winter vacation did not start off the right way. Gina and Danny were hanging out at the front door with their gaggle of sheep. I know that sheep are flocks and geese a gaggle but that's how I think of them. As an unmanaged gaggle following the slightest whim of the queen sheep.

Danny was letting his hair grow out now that football was finished. Starting to curl at the back, the deep reddish brown hair looked like it'd been recently ruffled by Gina. She looked her typical perfect self in a black skirt and white blouse. It's funny, but I don't remember her being this put together last year. This was a girl who'd definitely come into her own, found her niche at the top of the heap and would do anything to stay there.

She glanced my way and her eyes narrowed into a frown that could send a shiver through a great white shark. I'd never felt so hated before. Not even during the bad time. Then, I was simply something to be used. This was a conscious hate. My choice to support Scott reminded everyone what she'd done. How it must eat at her insides to not control everyone's thoughts. It made me smile back at her.

She turned away and whispered something to Nichol who looked my way as she listened to Gina. Nichol's face drained of all color and she shook her head. Obviously she was not fully onboard.

I dropped my head and tried to circle around the group blocking the hallway. The inconsiderate bastards didn't seem to care that they were backing up traffic and that there were hundreds of kids stomping their feet to shake off the cold while they waited.

Suddenly, Danny Carrs stood before me, stopping me in my tracks. He didn't say anything but his eyes traveled over my face and body. It wasn't in a sexual way.

Believe me I know the difference. But a curious expectant look that seemed to catalog each feature. He didn't smile, didn't leer. I wasn't pretty enough for that. Even in my wonderful new wool coat, I didn't come up to his standards.

Waiting for him to finish, I wanted to slap that sloppy grin that'd popped up. What made him think he had the right?

"Do you want something, or are you looking for something new already," I said, glancing to Gina a dozen feet away, deep in conversation with Nichol. She heard me, her head shot around to watch us, a scowl pinching her face in disgust and maybe a hint of fear.

"If I was, believe me, you'd be the last person on earth I'd be interested in." he answered.

"Thank you," I said and laughed. "That is one of the nicest things anyone has ever said to me."

He didn't react, didn't talk, just waited for me to figure out what was going on. I don't know how long we'd have stood there, probably until sometime in May but Scott walked through the door and the entire dynamic of the hallway changed. Standing head and shoulders above everyone else. People couldn't miss him.

I felt the air change, my shoulders tingled for a moment and I knew he was near. Everyone else's gaze followed his every movement as he pushed his way through the crowd.

He stepped next to me and the tension ratcheted up a million degrees. They hadn't worried about me. Scott was another thing altogether, I realized that they were afraid of him. Not just in a physical way, there was too many of them for that. No they also feared his moral superiority and the fact that he didn't care what the queen and king said or did.

He scanned the crowd and I could see his mind processing and figuring out what was going on. He sighed and pushed his way through the crowd and stepped next to me. Gently touching my elbow, he cocked an eyebrow asking me if everything was okay. I nodded and felt him relax.

Turning towards Danny he smiled and said, "What's going on, you guys talking to us now?" Turning to me he said, "I've told you as dozen times Katie, be careful who you are seen talking with. The wrong people can really impact your social status." Then laughed and started me down the hall.

Leave it to him to quickly and totally diffuse the situation. He'd shifted it off me and onto them like a Jujitsu move or something. It was beautiful.

All thoughts of Danny and Gina disappeared. All I could think about was the guy next to me. Was he having second thoughts about us going to the dance? A quick glance didn't give me anything. It was eating my insides, he couldn't have been serious. Why did he ask, did he feel sorry for me. I didn't know what he really thought about my mom and stuff. If he thought he was in social hell now. Imagine what it'd be like if everybody else found out about her. I would be a pariah throughout the town not just here in school.

"So are you looking forward to the dance?" he asked. I swear he could read my mind.

My books where held next to my chest as I walked next to him. I'd left my book bag at home; it didn't go with my new jacket. "Yes I am," I answered please to hear that I didn't sound too desperate.

"Good," he said his voice strong and firm as he held my first period door open for me.

For the rest of the morning, Scott was outside my class door and escorted me to my next class. My heart would race every time I saw him. I found myself thinking about Scott instead of my classes. Thankfully, the teachers were so used to not calling on me; I was able to slide through the day until lunch.

Once again Scott was waiting for me. My face flushed when I saw him, I wasn't used to all this attention. He wasn't possessive or crowding me, I knew he was doing it to protect me from getting hassled by the clique.

The cafeteria during lunch was loud like normal, things didn't go all quiet when we walked in, not like is used to. Scott followed me into the line and loaded his tray with three sandwiches, a couple of hard boiled eggs and piece of apple pie. The man could eat. I grabbed a salad and a yogurt from the refrigerator.

Scott jumped ahead of me in line and paid for both of our meals. I couldn't believe it. A little part of me was pleased, another part was mad. Did he think I couldn't afford it? What was going on? I started to tell him he shouldn't do it but he shook his head and shot a look at the cashier. Don't let them know his look said. Don't let them see your emotions. I accepted his gift and mumbled thanks.

Mattie and Kevin were already at our normal table. The student body had collectively decided to never use that table unless they become infected with our social sickness. Their heads were together in some kind of intense discussion. Both of them stopped talking when we walked up.

I sat next to Scott before I thought about how it would look. Hey, it was the least I could do, the guy did buy me lunch.

Mattie looked real cute in a fitted striped blouse. Her hair was down and not in its normal pony tail.

"Are you going to the dance next week?" I asked her. If she was going, maybe she could fill me in on what people wore. Plus, there would be someone there to talk to besides Scott. A nervous feeling fluttered through my stomach whenever I thought about the dance.

"Yes," Mattie said.

"No," Scott answered.

"You're not my father," Mattie said, her brow narrowing in a frown. I could tell that Scott had upset her, but I also knew she wasn't going to give in easy. Scott was in for a hell the next two weeks. I would be careful of my dinner if I was him.

He ignored her and started un-wrapping his sandwiches. Kevin looked back and forth between brother and sister but wisely stayed out of it.

"That's a shame, I was hoping you could help me figure out what to wear," I said.

Mattie's hand froze half way to her mouth. "You're going?" Obviously Scott hadn't told her. Why? Was he embarrassed? I wanted to shout about it from the school rooftop.

"Yes, we're going," Scott said as he took a bite from his sandwich.

Mattie's hand with her apple fell back to the table. Kevin smiled then folded his arms across his chest and leaned back waiting for the show.

"You're going, but I can't? You think it is perfectly okay for Katie, but not me."

"Katie's an adult, she can decide for herself, you on the other hand are not yet sixteen. No way is Grandfather letting you go, especially not after I talk to him."

Kevin and I both scooted on our benches to give them room. I dreaded the coming explosion. Mattie narrowed her eyebrows and stared at her brother as if she wanted to push a dagger through his heart then carve it out and lay it on the floor so she could jump on it a couple of times.

Her scowl deepened as she leaned forward. "You listen to me Scott O'Brian James, you aren't the boss of me and you need to stay out of my business or you will live to regret it. Do you hear me?" With that she picked up her lunch and stomped from the table. Kevin looked at both of us and shrugged his shoulders before he jumped to follow her.

"Well, that went better than I thought it would," Scott said, shaking his head.

"Do you really think you can stop her from going?" I asked.

"No of course not. Nobody has ever stopped Mattie from doing what she wants to. Luckily she doesn't push it. No way can I keep her from going."

"Then why, if you hold too tight you'll end up driving her away." My thoughts jumped to my mom, is that what had happened to her.

"I know, but I've got to let her know there are limits. She's going to push up against them, even step over the line occasionally. But if I don't set 'em, she won't ever know when something is too far out of bounds."

Shaking my head I returned to my salad and tried to figure it out.

"Besides," he continued. "It's sort of fun pissing her off every so often. That's what big brothers are for, pushing buttons, and beating the crap out of any guy that touches her."

## Chapter Twelve

<u>Scott</u>

Mattie wasn't kind enough to give me the silent treatment. The girl didn't know the meaning of the word. It was relentless. All of my many short comings constantly being discussed and emphasized. I tried tuning her out but like I said she was relentless.

Ten days of banging pots and pissed off stares. I was very relieved when the day of the dance finally arrived. Mattie would get over it tomorrow and put it behind her.

I tightened my tie's knot and slipped on my suit jacket. It felt a little tighter across the shoulders. I wondered if I would I ever stop growing? A quick glance in the front mirror confirmed everything looked okay. My stomach tumbled. I don't know why I was so nervous. It was just a high school dance. Gathering myself I looked for Mattie but couldn't find her anywhere, she was probably out in the barn pouting. Telling Chrissy and Star about what a terrible brother she had.

Deciding to leave her alone, I grabbed the flowers I'd gotten earlier in the morning and told Grandfather goodbye. He looked up from his paper and gave me the once over. Obviously meeting with his approval he nodded his head. "You're taking her flowers?" he asked.

"Yes sir, it's not a formal thing, so guys don't give the girls corsages or anything, but I thought I'd take her some flowers anyway. I picked up a pretty bouquet at the grocery store this morning."

"Okay, you have a good time and tell Katie I said hi."

It felt strange driving off without saying bye to Mattie.

.o0o.

I rang the doorbell and unconsciously held my breath. Her Aunt Jenny answered the door and invited me inside. She had a huge smile as she looked me over and nodded her head in approval. Her eyes got a little misty and I wondered if my dad had ever taken her to a school dance. Had he stood in this very spot and waited with sweating palms and racing heart like I was now.

"Katie will be here in a minute, let me go get her," she said then turned and left.

My tie felt like it would choke me to death; how come it kept getting tighter the longer I wore it. Putting my finger between my collar and neck I pulled and tried to get some breathing room. I looked at my dress shoes and realized I'd picked up gunk somewhere along the way and quickly wiped them on the back of my cuffs.

A sudden electric shock in the air made me look up and catch the vision of an angel in black. Katie stood before me in the sexiest dress ever worn. My mouth went dry and I forgot how to speak. I couldn't help myself as my eyes traveled over her, taking in every detail. She wore a simple black dress that hugged every curve and ended at mid-thigh. Black high heels with ankle straps highlighted long luscious legs in panty hose. I pulled my eyes back towards her face but I couldn't stop myself from staring at her narrow waist and curved hips. Her breasts showed a lot of cleavage but managed to seem chaste and pure at the same time.

Her hair was up in some king of sexy French twist thing and she wore a black ribbon chocker necklace with a small ivory cameo. I swear my heart had forgotten to beat for several seconds then it let go and couldn't stop. She was the most beautiful thing I'd ever seen. She wasn't wearing her glasses and I wondered if she was using contacts. Her makeup was subtle but highlighted every one of her many outstanding features. The effect was entrancing. I couldn't pull my eyes away and couldn't think what to say.

"Uhm, you look amazing," I finally got out, breaking the ice.

She blushed and looked down while saying "thank you." Her voice sounded like angel wings brushing a cloud.

I think I'd have stood there admiring Katie for the rest of the night but Aunt Jenny coughed interrupting my thoughts. She stood to the side, a hand hiding a smile as she looked between Katie and me. This time I was sure I could see a tear in her eyes.

"Are those for me?" Katie asked indicating the flowers in my hand.

"Uhm yes, I uhm got them for you." Of course I had, how idiotic was I going to be tonight. This is ridiculous, get yourself together Scott. I took a deep breath and stepped forward and handed her the flowers. It surprised me that my feet remembered how to move.

She took the flowers in both hands and brought them to her face and took a deep breath, pulling in the scent. She smile back at me and I thought my heart would melt. My god she was so beautiful. She'd always been pretty but this was so much more. I couldn't wait to walk into the gym with this girl on my arm. Every guy in the place was going to kick themselves for not paying her any attention before this.

Almost immediately that thought was followed by the realization of what every other guy in the place would be imagining once they saw her in that dress. I was going to have to work hard not to pound their bulging eyes back into their heads. Maybe she'd be willing to keep her jacket on all night. I wanted to be the only one who ever saw her like this.

She handed the flowers to Aunt Jenny and asked her to put them in water then leaned forward and whispered something to her ear. Jenny nodded as she wiped an eye.

Katie smiled at her aunt and asked if I was ready?

I nodded, lost in looking at her. I finally remembered my manners and took her long wool coat from the coat rack and held it for her to put on. She slipped her arms in then turned to look up at me. Her eyes got very serious for a moment. She looked deep into my eyes as if trying to figure out the secrets of the world. I wondered what she saw and found myself starting to fall into her deep green eyes.

"Thank you for tonight," She said. "No matter what, thank you." She reached up and straitened my tie then brushed a piece of lint from my shoulders. An electric shock sparked where she touched me. We smiled at each other and an unspoken commitment passed between us. We would go through tonight together. Face it as a team, and enjoy ourselves while doing it.

"Before we go, this is for you," she said pulling a small tissue paper wrapped package from her tiny black purse. Surprised out of my skull I slowly opened the present. A white handkerchief with a beautiful letter *S* embroidered in cobalt blue rested in the paper. My brow furrowed in confusion and I looked at her for an explanation.

"It's the one you used on my locker. I'd have got it back to you sooner if it hadn't taken forever to get that ugly red out of it. That and the fact that it took me longer than planned to get the S just right."

Thunderstruck doesn't begin to explain how I felt as I put the handkerchief into my inside suit pocket and followed her out.

I held the truck door open and helped her in. A flash of leg exposed itself and my pulse pumped a thousand times. I had to fight to get myself back under control. I've got to admit that all I wanted to do was take her somewhere and make sweet love to her all night long and again all day tomorrow.

.o0o.

Katie

My heart felt like it would pound out of my chest, Scott was so handsome in his suit, he'd gotten a haircut and his subtle aftershave washed over me with a slight smoky musk smell that turned my insides to mush. I will never forget the look on his face when he first saw me. The admiration and let's admit it, lust. Had sent a shiver up my spine and turned me into a quivering mess. I shot a glance his ways from under my brow admiring his wide shoulders and gorgeous face. He looked nervous as he focused on the road.

A quick check confirmed my handy wipes in my jacket pocket. I'd placed them there earlier but swore to myself that I wouldn't use them. They were there so I wouldn't focus on their absence. I focused on my hands in my lap instead and wondered if this was all real.

The tension between us continued to build as neither of us broke the silence. It was different than normal. I don't know why but it felt like something had changed the moment he saw me in this dress.

Scott cleared his throat and smiled at me. "You're not wearing your glasses?" he said.

"Contacts," I said. "I don't normally like them, can't stand putting them in or taking them out but I didn't think glasses went with this dress." I said.

Scott nodded and smiled. I was sure he was thinking back to what I looked like. I remembered the tingly feel when his eyes had traveled up and down my body and was shocked that I hadn't been hurt or embarrassed, or even disgusted. I had enjoyed it immensely.

"Yeah, Danny used to be the same way until his vanity over-ruled his survival instinct," Scott said. It took me a moment to realize we were talking about contacts and glasses.

As we left his truck and started towards the front door I wobbled a little on my high heels. How women wore these every day I will never know, but I had to admit I liked the way they made me look. Scott reached over to

# Certain Rules

place my hand through his arm and made sure to match my pace as I picked my way across the uneven ground.

He patted my hand with his other hand and smiled down at me with that heart stopping little boy grin. "We are going to piss them off and totally ruin their perfect night. Whatever happens, don't let them get you down. Shake it off and enjoy yourself.

I smiled back but couldn't answer. I don't know when I'd ever been more nervous. Afraid yes, but not nervous like this.

Scott handed our tickets to Mrs. Layther who was manning the door. We stepped in and he helped me off with my coat. My face grew flushed when I immediately felt the stares and whispered comments.

"Why are they here?"

"Look at that dress" A junior girl sneered.

"Yeah, look," her date said and several of the boys in the vicinity chuckled.

Scott handed my coat to a freshman girl manning the coat check station telling her to make sure nothing happened to it. He gave her a look that would have scared a German shepherd, let alone an un-cool freshman girl. She nodded and carefully placed it aside and handed him a printed number.

We turned and entered the gym together. He took my hand in his. A cool calm strength passed into me and I knew that I could do anything with this man next to me.

The gym was decorated in balloons and crepe paper banners. It was sort of cheesy but what were you going to do in Nebraska in the winter. A silver disco ball hung from the ceiling. Lit by spot lights it threw sparkly colors throughout the room. I thought everything was perfect and exactly like I'd imagined it. The band was tuning up and getting ready.

"We'd normally have to take our shoes off before going in, but they're going to refinish the floor this summer so we lucked out," Scott said.

I tried to swallow.

Scott saw my nervousness and leaned down to whisper in my ear. His breath tickled and sent warm shivers up and down my back. "You are the sexiest most beautiful woman here. All the guys will want you and all the women will wish they were you. But remember you came with me so don't get any ideas about dumping me for one of these other jerks."

I couldn't help myself and laughed. He always knew the perfect thing to say. We walked across the gym floor hand in hand. The sea of bodies parted to let us through. I ignored the stares and comments and focused on how wonderful my hand felt in his.

We made it to the other side then turned to watch the crowd. The cool kids were too stunned to mutter to each other. Gina stared daggers and John's mouth seemed to have forgotten how to close. Nichole elbowed him the ribs to bring him back to reality. I made sure they all saw me staring at them then smiled and turned my back.

The band started off with a song by Green Day. Soon everyone had forgotten about us and started pairing up and dancing. Most of the boys were in suits, a few simply in dress shirts and ties. The girls in dresses and heels.

Scott hadn't let go of my hand as he looked out over everyone. He glanced at me and cocked an eyebrow. "Do you want to dance?" he asked.

My heart skipped a beat as I nodded yes then followed as he led me out onto the dance floor. The heavy beat flowed through me as the music took over and let myself go.

For such a big man he danced well, smoothly and with a firm sense of rhythm.  The people around us gave us plenty of room and I felt like we were in our own little world where nothing could ruin it. We were half way into the second song when Scott froze in place and looked across the huge gym, his brow creased in a deep frown. I stopped and looked over my shoulder. Mattie had entered the gym with her best friend Mary Wilson.

Scott scowled but didn't move for a moment, He seemed to remember where he was and smiled at me and shrugged his shoulders as if to say, what are you going to do?

I let out a breath and realized I'd been dreading the thing that was going to ruin the evening, waiting for that incident that would destroy my night. It was hard for me to believe that it might not happen, that things might be okay after all.

The song ended and Scott took my hand and started to lead me over to where Mattie and a bunch of her friends were gathered. They backed away as we approached leaving Mattie all alone to face her brother. Before we could get there, Kevin appeared next to her side and whispered in her ear. She laughed and turned to confront Scott. Her shoulders gathered themselves and I could tell she was preparing for battle.

She bit her lip as Scott stopped in front of her and examined her close. Taking in the earrings and makeup and her slinky silk blue dress that matched her sky blue eyes. She looked like a young girl taking her first steps into the adult world. Please don't ruin it for her I prayed and squeezed his hand.

He continued to scowl then his eyes relaxed and he smiled. "You look very nice Mattie," he said. "Will you save me a dance for later?"

Mattie seemed to deflate as if all the steam had been let out of a pressure cooker. She smiled and nodded her head then threw herself into her brother's arms and gave him the biggest hug this side of Kansas.

A tear threatened to leak from my eyes but I was able to wipe it away without messing up my makeup.

Mattie stepped back from her brother and smiled at me. Her eyes grew huge when she saw me in my new dress and she hugged me. "You look dangerous," She said.

"I'll say," Kevin added.

Within moments we are all talking at the same time and the group was back. What would I ever do without these people? Please don't let anything screw it up.

## Chapter Thirteen
### Scott

I'd almost screwed things up with Mattie. The fact that I'd desperately wanted to make sure I didn't look like a jerk in front of Katie had seriously impacted how I reacted. And it seemed to have been the right move. Even if it went against every bit of my soul to let these two out in public looking as good as they looked at the moment.

The band had started and Kevin asked Mattie to dance. Her eyes lit up like fireworks as she beamed all the way onto the floor. Katie looked over at me then grabbed my hand to pull me out on the floor. I laughed and let her drag me back out there.

We'd finished another song and I could feel the room growing warmer as the evening got into full swing. I held her hand as we waited for the band to start its next number when the female singer approached the microphone and started to belt out the Eta James classic 'AT LAST'. The ultimate romantic slow song.

My heart dropped as I looked at Katie, She'd probably feel real uncomfortable slow dancing with me. The top of her head didn't reach my chin. We'd look like the Jolly Green Giant and Little Green Sprout on the dance floor. Besides there was that -whole not liking to be touched- thing. She wasn't near as jumpy as she used to be but there were still an occasional flinch.

What if the thought of me holding her disgusted her? I'd never do anything to make her feel that way. Okay Scott, you're over thinking things, relax and play it through.

A sly look escaped from under her brow. Her eyes were big and glittering as she waited for me to come to some kind of decision. I took a deep breath and asked "Would you dance with me Ms. Rivers?" I figured if I made it a formal request she was less likely to say no. Besides, if she did turn me down, I could always try and turn it into a joke.

She smiled and came into my arms like she'd always belonged there. Resting her head on my chest she placed her hands on my shoulders and followed my lead as we slowly swayed to the music. There was a god and I'd found heaven.

Her hair smelt of jasmine and honeysuckle. A sweat scent that burnt its way to my very core and seared itself into my long term memory. I closed my eyes and got lost in the feeling of wonderment. She felt so soft and tender in my arms. Of their own free will my hands drifted down her back to rest just above her bottom. I had to consciously stop them from reaching lower and squeezing.

She felt so warm, and soft, and curvy. All I could do was think about her body next to mine. I blanked out everything around me except the music and her.

My body betrayed me and started to get aroused for the thousandth time that night. A shock of embarrassment shot through me as I wondered how she'd react. Maybe if I prayed real hard she wouldn't notice. Of course I wasn't so lucky, there was no way she could avoid noticing as I felt myself grow hard against her stomach. As I shifted to put some room between us and give her an opportunity to escape she moaned and pulled me closer.

Heaven had just become Nirvana.

.oOo.

<u>Katie</u>

There is such a thing as bliss. A safe, secure place, free of stress or fear. A place where a person could feel like they were supposed to feel, happy and full of wonderment that the world is good and just. Inside Scott's arms while we danced was my place.

I discovered it that night when I rested my head on his chest. A relaxing peace filled my body as I inhaled his scent. For the first time since I could remember I felt that all was right with the world. When my mind started to drift to bad times and bad memories I was able to push them aside and focus on the here and now.

His heart marched in time with the drum beats, making me smile. He felt so big and strong. So solid and all there. A powerful ache blossomed deep inside of me. A burning need that I'd never known before and feared I'd never know.

My heart soared with the realization that I wasn't broken, wasn't ruined forever. I became very aware of his body, his hands resting on my lower back, his beating heart, and his warm man smell. All of it sent small electric shocks directly to my spine and my lower tummy.

He shifted trying to put some distance between us and I moaned at the thought of losing this sense of being surrounded by him. I felt his hardness next to my stomach and my face flushed red. That was why he moved.

I tensed up as I waited for my body to rebel. Waited for my mind to freak out and embarrass us both. But it didn't happen that way. Instead, my insides turned soft and a burning desire consumed me. My hands drifted up to clasp behind his neck. It was as if someone had cut away the shackles that had been binding me for years. I was free to feel, to want, to need.

The song ended and we slowly separated. I felt a physical loss and emptiness. I looked into his face and tried to catch a glimpse of what he was thinking, what he was feeling. Had it affected him like it had me? I know the physical signs were there but I desperately wanted to know what was going through his mind.

He smiled and gave me a hug as he kissed the top of my head. "You and I are going to have to talk, but not here, not now. Let's just enjoy the rest of the evening," he said.

My shoulders relaxed and I leaned into him. He did get it, it was important to him. I flashed to that time three years earlier. My stomach dropped, I was going to have to tell him I realized. Telling him about my mom had been hard enough. How could I ever face him once he knew the truth? How could I ever face him if I kept it from him?

Kevin and Mattie joined us and the moment was broken and lost. Instead we spent the rest of the night dancing and laughing. Scott pulled Mattie onto the floor for a Styx song and Kevin asked me to dance. The four of us ended up in our own little world in the middle of the dance floor. Everyone and everything forgotten.

Much later we were standing off to the side talking and taking a break when a sophomore, Mark Johansson approached and shot Scott a nervous look. He smiled weakly at me and asked me to dance. You could have dropped me through a threshing mill I was so surprised.

Scott stepped forward with a deep scowl and his fists clenched but he didn't say anything. I looked at him and placed a hand flat on his chest and raised an eyebrow in question. I know I didn't have to get his permission, but for some reason I thought it was important. He reluctantly nodded and stepped back.

I smiled at Mark and said, "Are you sure?"

"Are you home schooled?" Kevin asked him. Mattie elbowed him in the ribs and he looked at her with an innocent expression as if to say "What?"

The young boy blushed and said, "Yes, I'm sure and no I'm not home schooled. I know what everybody is going to say."

Shooting Scott a smile, I followed Mark to the dance floor. It wasn't the same as dancing with Scott. Mark didn't have the smooth athletic movement nor the overwhelming presence. It was fun though, especially the look of raw jealousy that resided on Scotts face. A girl could live off that for months.

When the song ended Mark escorted me back to the group and nodded towards Scott, thanked me then turned and left. People didn't turn their backs on him, but I noticed there were a lot of hard stares.

"He must have lost a bet," Kevin said as we watched him walk away.

Mattie elbowed him again.

"Damn that hurts, what I'd do this time?" he asked.

"You have the brains of a frog, and that's being mean to frogs everywhere." She said as she shook her head.

"Don't be too hard on him, he's probably right," I said. Not minding at all. I was having a wonderful night.

"I know exactly what happened," Scott said with that air of authority he gets when he wants to pretend he knows what's going on. The three of us looked at him expectantly. "The guy's a bit of a nerd and geek, he isn't on any of the sports teams. He's never been very popular."

"What's that go to do with it?" Mattie asked. "Even the unpopular kids aren't going to risk the hazing if they don't have to."

"It's simple, when he left home tonight he promised himself he was going to ask the most beautiful girl in the room to dance. Once he saw Katie, he had no choice in the matter. The issue was resolved no other girl could compete."

"Hey!" Mattie said with a small teasing pout.

"Obviously he couldn't ask you to dance Mattie, Kevin would have kicked his ass," Scott said then slapped the other boy on the back. Kevin blushed but didn't deny it. Mattie grew very red and suddenly silent.

We all laughed but a warm glow filled me. Okay, the night could get better. The fact that I was going to have to ruin it later by telling Scott the truth about my past weighed on me like a ton of bricks. I think Scott noticed but he didn't say anything. Letting me have my night of joy.

The gym grew warm but other than a few breaks we danced all night. Boy, that's a phrase I never thought

I'd use. There were several more slow dances and each was better than the last. My whole body was flushed and my heart raced a thousand miles a minute.

When we were leaving Scott retrieved my coat and asked me to wait while he took Mattie and her friend Mary to her mom's car. Kevin stepped forward and said he'd do it. Mattie blushed and shot her brother a look of command. I placed my hand on his arm trying to send him a message to let Kevin walk with her. He got it and relaxed. "Okay," was all he said. Mattie beamed and gave me a hug before joining Mary and shooting Kevin a glance full of hidden meaning.

Scott watched them walk out and shook his head. "She's not following the rule about little sisters not being allowed to grow up."

I laughed and hugged his arm as we walked to his truck. The cold air bit into any exposed flesh and seemed to sap the sweat right off of me. Within about twenty two seconds I was shivering. Scott put his arm around me and pulled me into one of his patented hugs.

When we go to his truck he held my door opened and helped me up. High heels and dresses are not meant for climbing in and out of trucks. He stood there for a moment holding the door open. "You know, the beauty of a bench seat in a truck is that people can sit in the middle if they want."

My brow creased in confusion, what was he talking about.

"I'm just saying, it might be warmer for you."

His face was starting to turn a little red, why would he worry about me getting warm, the truck heater would have everything toasty within seconds. Or at least it would if he'd hurry and shut my door and get in and start it up. It struck me, he wanted me to sit next to him.

Now it was my time to blush. That was the kind of thing a girlfriend did, not just a date. Bless it girl, I thought, get your butt over there before he changes his mind. I smiled back up at him and nodded as I slid across the seat. Scott raced around and jumped in.

That kind of truck has both of the female ends of the buckles next to each other. Somehow we got buckled into each other's set and laughed as our hands got all tangled up. I wouldn't have changed it for anything.

"Are you in a hur…."

"Do we have to…." We both said at the same time

"No we don't have to go home right away. In fact, I'd like to show you something if you're not in a rush." Scott said. Then asked if I had a good time.

"I had a wonderful time, thank you so much," I said but couldn't keep a frown from appearing when I remembered what I had to tell him. I'd have to do it soon, but maybe not tonight. I could put it off one more day couldn't I?

"What's wrong?" he asked, obviously having caught my frown.

I shook my head and said, "I was just sad thinking that this night would have to end and we'd have to go back to being our normal selves."

"It's not over yet," he said as he pulled into the long line of cars waiting to exit the school parking lot. The car behind headlights shown through the truck cab and I realized that everybody would see me sitting next to Scott James in his truck. This seemed even more special than holding hands or dancing slow on the gym floor. This was serious and I couldn't stop smiling.

## Chapter Fourteen

<u>Scott</u>

I drove out of town thinking about the girl next to me. What was going on in that beautiful head of hers? Things had changed between us and I think she knew it. "What are you thinking about," I asked.

Katie hesitated for moment then looked up and smiled. "You."

"Me, what about me?"

"Oh, wondering if you're going to get a big head after you learn how good a job you did tonight, making it all special."

I chuckled but didn't say anything else. I could wait until we got there. She stiffened next to me when I slowed down and pulled off onto a dirt road. She looked at me with expectant eyes but I kept quiet and focused on the road. The moon ducked behind some clouds and my headlights were all I had to follow on the twisting trail up the hill. I downshifted for that last little bit and pulled up on the bluff.

The moon chose that exact moment to come out and illuminate the valley before us. It looked like someone had laid a crisp white sheet across the farmland and was shining a silver spot light through the night. Little yellow twinkly lights dotted the floor of the valley indicating the occasional farm house. In the far distance a car's red rear lights was moving away from us. Probably one of the kids returning home after the dance.

Katie gasped when she saw it. Her admiration and pleasure sent a sharp thrill through me. I casually draped an arm around her shoulders and pulled her close. She slipped an arm behind my back and nuzzled into my side. Both of us watched the scenery. I knew I was delaying things but I was enjoying myself to much.

"You said we needed to talk," she said without lifting her head from my side.

There comes a time in everybody's life when you have to face something that scares the crap out of you. In reality, I hadn't come across that many things that scare me. Not until that night.

Letting out a big sigh, I swallowed hard and prepared to tell her how much I liked her and hoped like hell she liked me back. I wasn't ready to broach the whole love subject, but I'll be honest it was there in the back of my mind.

Before I could get started, Katie said, "I need to tell you something."

My stomach dropped, I'd feared this for a while.

.oOo.

<u>Katie</u>

When you love someone you should be honest with them. I'd learned that much from my mom. Her lies had hurt us much more than her actions. The fact that I was madly and hopelessly in love with Scott James did not come as a big shock to me. My heart felt like it was going to explode with happiness, I loved Scott and it didn't scare me. Well not too much anyway.

# Certain Rules

I couldn't put this off any longer. He deserved to know what he was getting himself into. It was the least I could do for him after everything he'd done for me tonight. My heart raced and I was sure he could feel it pounding into his ribs as I clung to his side.

"Something happened three years ago. I need to tell you about it," I said.

He tensed up; I think he knew it was bad. Being Scott he squeezed my shoulder letting me know that he was there if I needed him.

"I told you about my mom, but I didn't tell you everything. She started out as a high priced escort. I think she'd some wild scheme to become a movie star but flamed out like every other young girl in southern California. Her life never crossed into mine except for keeping everything a secret. If that'd been it everything could have gone on. No big deal, I mean, every teenage girl has a sucky life right."

"Yeah, I guess," he said with a little catch in his throat.

"As you might imagine, she kept getting older and started sliding down the harlot pecking order. She had a regular list of clients but they weren't enough." I chuckled, I couldn't believe I was talking about her like she was a clinical psychologist or something.

"She fell in with some real bad people." I took a deep breath; this was where it got hard.

"One day a guy named Jimmy showed up at our door. I shouldn't have let him in but I knew he was her boyfriend and/or pimp, depending upon your definition of boyfriend. I'd seen him pick her up some times in his fancy convertible." I stopped here and tried to catch my breath. The memories were flooding back in and I couldn't keep them out. A tear spilled over and dripped down my cheek. Burying my face into Scott's jacket I tried to get lost.

"You don't have to do this if you don't want to. I'm here for whatever you want but you don't owe me anything," he said.

"Oh, but I do Scott, I owe you more than you will ever know. I need to tell you this. Nobody else really knows the whole story. I think Aunt Jenny has some ideas. But I've never told anyone everything."

He squeezed my shoulder again me giving the confidence to go on.

"Jimmy was looking for my mom and was really upset when he found out she wasn't there. Supposedly she owed him a whole bunch of money. He went through the house opening doors and yelling her name. The man made my skin crawl and I wanted him out of our there so I grabbed his arm. It was like grabbing a telephone pole. He looked at me and I think that was the first time he really saw me. He got this nasty sneer and said that my mom owed him a lot of money but that I could start making a down payment."

"His eyes were like a lizard's, small and beady and they never blinked. They burnt a hole in my soul. My stomach dropped and I ran for the door. If I could get to Mrs. Carlucci's I'd be okay. But he caught me at the door and dragged me back into the living room. I screamed but he hit me in the face." My hand drifted up to rub my jaw. I could still feel the blinding pain as it shot through my head. "I'd never been hit before," I said as if that made any difference.

"He raped me, there on the living room floor."

Scott was so still, I don't think his heart had beaten since I'd started. "I am so sorry Katie, I wish with all my heart you didn't have to go through that." I could feel his fist clench in my coat.

"There's more. When he was done, he started yelling at me for not telling him I was a virgin. He kept saying how much he could have gotten for my first time. He started hitting me again then he raped me again. I wanted to die. If I could of I would have killed myself right then and there."

Scott started to say something but I held my fingers to his lips. "Let me finish, I have to get this out."

He nodded against my fingers.

"He made me change into new cloths. He stood there and watched the whole time as I got dressed." I sniffled but took another breath, I had to finish this. "He grabbed my neck and showed me a knife. He said if I gave him any problems he'd kill me then find my mom and kill her too."

"I'd stopped thinking by that point. I let him lead me out of the apartment building. I didn't struggle, didn't try to escape. I just let him pull me to his car. We drove to an old converted warehouse. He threw me into a bedroom and told me that I was his now and that I'd do what he told me with whoever he found. If I didn't he'd slice me into a thousand pieces." I could remember the cold steel of his knife sliding up and down my skin.

"Well to make a long story short, for the next two weeks he kept me locked up in that room. Coming back every day, sometimes twice. I didn't fight him, I didn't try to escape. It was like I was dead inside. I don't know how long he would have kept me there. Maybe until I was awake enough to kill myself.

"He didn't show up for a few days. He got busted for assaulting one of my mother's customers. After a couple of days of him not showing up I finally came out of it enough to escape. I kicked at the door until it opened. I thought for sure somebody would throw me back in. The place was empty though. I grabbed a dirty sheet off the bed and ran outside. A cop found me wondering around and the rest is history as they say."

Scott felt like a solid rock in a raging torrent. He was the only thing I could think of, my only awareness. Desperately I waited for his response. Would he push me away in disgust, or simply turn and drive me home to be abandoned to my fear and shame. The waiting was driving me insane and pushing my beating heart to the breaking point. A deadly silence enveloped our little world marred by my sniffles and the gentle hiss of the heater fan on the dashboard.

He shifted and my heart stopped for a moment. He brought his other arm around me and pulled me into the deepest warmest hug of my life. He kissed the top of my head "I'm sorry, so sorry honey, I'm sorry." He kept mumbling into my hair while he stroked my back.

The damn broke as my muscles relaxed and I started to cry, truly ball my eyes out and it felt wonderful. As if a pent up pressure cooker that had been left on high heat for three years had finally burst through the safety valve. Everything was released as I cried into his arms. Scott rocked me and kept telling me he was sorry and that everything was going to be okay now. He had me, I was safe here.

"It's not your fault you know," he said as he held me, caressing the back of my head.

That set me off again into another crying jag. No one had ever told me that before. Not the nurses at the hospital, not the police, no one. To have him be the first made it all that more special. I could almost believe it if he was saying it. I mumbled an "I know,"

His suit jacket was now sopping wet, probably ruined. I pulled back but his arms clamped down and held on for a few seconds longer before letting me go. I looked up to his face. Everything was cast in silver shadows but he couldn't hide the hurt and anger. Knowing that he was angry at others and hurt for me did more to heal my soul than anything to that point.

"I need to know what you're feeling, not thinking, feeling," I said.

He hesitated a moment, "It's hard for me to talk about my feelings," he said.

"Nooooo really?" I said with a chuckle. It felt good to break the tension a little.

He laughed, but the look in his eyes didn't change. They looked out over our beautiful valley. Lost in thought for a moment.

He took a deep breath and said. "I'm feeling a dozen different things. My max used to be three." He gave me a weak smile. "I'm angry that you were ever put in that situation. Obviously angry at your attacker, angry that I can't get my hands on him this moment and end his miserable life. I'm angry at myself for not being there to

# Certain Rules

save you. It feels like I failed you somehow. I know it was long before we met, but still, I should have done something. My heart is broken for your hurt and pain. The fact that you have been carrying this around all alone makes me a little mad at you, but also a little admiring of your strength and courage. I am scared to death that I am going to do or say something stupid and hurt you more. "

Wow, I didn't know a guy could feel that many things at once. The silver moonlight cast his face in a black and white shadow like a 1940's movie. With that sweet little scar and piercing eyes. If you made him wear a fedora he'd look like one of those hard bitten detectives, a Robert Mitchum type. The kind of guy with a soft heart and iron soul.

"I'm feeling tons of things," he continued. "But I know something for sure. I know that I love you, probably since you sat down at my lunch table like you could care less about what anybody thought. And I know that I will never let anything bad ever happen to you again."

My mouth fell open and my heart stopped beating. Did Scott James just tell me he loved me? This hard giant with a heart of gold said he loved me. After everything I'd told him, after laying out all my baggage. He says he loves me and wants to protect me. My insides melted and I fell into his arms thanking God for bringing such a person into my life.

I was so overwhelmed I didn't say a word. Finally I realized he probably wanted to hear me say something back. Guys are like that, they expose their innermost emotions. They sort of want to hear you love them back. The fact that I had loved him before I sat across from him in the cafeteria only made it easier. I pulled away to look into his eyes when I told him but he pressed a finger to my lips and shook his head as he pulled me back to his sides and turned us to stare out the front windshield at the black and white wonder world.

## Chapter Fifteen

<u>Scott</u>

My heart had shattered into a million pieces when Katie told me her story.

I could feel her chest rise with every breath as she slept next to me in my truck. Her Jasmine and Honeysuckle scent permeated the truck creating a soothing comforting place somehow. So different than the hell she'd told me about. It had been the most harrowing thing I'd ever heard. How did somebody put their life back together after something like that?

I gently rubbed her shoulder being careful not to wake her up. Smiling to myself as I remembered what it had felt like to tell her I loved her. That liberating and freeing feeling had washed over me when I'd admitted it to her and to myself.

Starting to stir, she whimpered in her sleep then blinked slowly as she opened her eyes. Her head bounced from side to side as she tried to place her surroundings then she saw me. Her eyes jumped all the way open and her hand immediately went to her mouth to make sure she hadn't drooled all over herself.

I laughed and said, "Good morning sunshine."

"What time is it?"

"Three A.M."

"What, you let me sleep. What's Aunt Jenny going to think?"

"She's going to think you're an eighteen year old woman. Besides I called her a couple of hours ago."

"What, what did you tell her?" she asked, her eyes as big as the full moon setting in the distance.

I was tempted to joke with her and say I'd told her aunt that we were spending the night at a motel and I'd have her home in a week or two but I didn't know what kind of mood she was in. I was scared shitless that I'd screw it up by saying the wrong thing. So I wisely decided to tell her the truth. "I told her that I'd taken you to the bluffs and that you'd fallen asleep."

Katie turned a beautiful shade of pink and locked on her hands folded in her lap.

"I'm sorry about that," she said. "What did Aunt Jenny say?"

"She said I should let you sleep. You didn't tell me you had a hard time sleeping."

"Believe me, I've told you enough to last you for a while."

I laughed and started my truck.

"What have you been doing, did you fall asleep too?"

"No I watched the scenery go by and held a beautiful girl in my arms as she slept. You don't snore by the way, just thought you should know."

"Of course I don't snore," she said as if the very idea was preposterous.

I placed the truck in gear but stopped and looked at her for a moment. "Listen I need you to do me a favor.

I'm a guy, if I screw up, say or do the wrong thing. You've got to let me know. Okay? It wasn't intentional."

Katie balked for a moment then smiled and nodded her head as she hugged my arm.

"I better get you home before your Aunt calls out the National Guard."

.oOo.

Katie

The ride home was quiet and peaceful. I couldn't believe he'd let me sleep like that. How embarrassing. He was probably being nice when he said I didn't snore. I'm sure I drooled all over myself. I didn't really care though. My heart was in heaven, a feeling of relief and wellbeing had settled over me. Scott had been an angel and I knew I was on the right road to living a normal life. It's amazing what baring one's soul could do for you.

We pulled into my drive way and I suddenly started to get nervous. Would he kiss me good night, What if he didn't? The poor guy had to feel like he was walking on egg shells around the broken girl. Scared the wrong step would send her over the edge. Heaven knew I hadn't done much to disabuse him of the idea.

He opened my door and I scooted across the seat. Aunt Jenny had left the porch light on. Walking to my front door felt like a march to the gallows. He didn't touch me and I didn't touch him. It was like the closeness between us had been forgotten and we'd returned to the world before the dance.

It was as if a high wall had sprung up between us. I swallowed hard and stopped on the porch to turn and look at him. He was two steps lower than me. Our eyes were even and that was with me in heals. I liked this view. It was nice staring into his chocolate brown eyes without having to crane my neck.

"You know," I said "It would be a big screw up to let me go in without a good night kiss."

He smirked, but I caught a quick flash of relief across his eyes.

"You always know the perfect thing to say," he said placing a hand on each of my hips sending a warm electric sizzle down my legs and up my spine. We stared into each other's eyes for a moment. He slowly brought his lips to mine and answered a burning question while he ignited a burning need.

His lips were firm but gentle as we caressed each other's mouth. My hands drifted to his neck and his to my lower back and I remembered the slow dance on the gym floor. My insides turned to mush again, every cell in my body wanted him, craved his touch. My heart raced and I reluctantly pushed away to catch my breath.

He smiled and said, "Good night, Katharine, sweet dreams."

Before he could turn and leave I grabbed his lapels and pulled him in close for another kiss. When we broke the clinch I held onto him and looked square into his eyes.

"I love you too Scott James," I said and squealed inside when I saw pure happiness leap into his eyes. He smiled and kissed me on the forehead and said he'd call me tomorrow.

"You better call me today," I yelled as he climbed into his truck. He laughed and waved then backed out into the street and idled there while he waited for me to go inside.

.oOo.

Scott did call me later that day. We talked for hours. Well really, I talked and he grunted occasionally to let me know he was still on the line. It was as if I couldn't be turned off. We talked about school, about the dance, about music, national politics, and of course sports. He told me about applying for student loans and several different scholarships.

When it came to end the call we both wanted the other to hang up first, it was sickening sweet and I loved every moment of it. He finally hung up and I laughed because I won. Of course, he called back thirty seconds later and said it was his turn to win and made me hang up first. Like I said sickening sweet.

It made me want to create a Facebook page just so I could mark "In a Relationship" on my profile page. I was his girlfriend wasn't I? I mean, he had asked me to sit in the middle seat of his truck hadn't he. Life was wonderful, me being me of course, I wondered what was going to ruin it all.

Scott picked me up in the morning before school and made Mattie get out so I could sit in the middle. She rolled her eyes but gave me a hug letting me know she was really okay with it. At the end of the day he'd drive Mattie all the way home then turn around and take me home. He said it was because he didn't want his little sister getting any ideas watching her big brother kissing his girlfriend. My heart jumped when he called me his girlfriend, is there any better word in the English language?

School was different. It even smelt different. Everything was stronger, fresher. The lunch room had fresh Chocolate chip cookies. The restrooms were awash with pine sol. The hallways sported new shiny wax jobs. Everything was new and unique.

We spent every free moment together. We'd walk down the middle of the hall hand in hand forcing everyone to give way so they wouldn't be seen interacting with the lepers. I noticed some of the stares from the other girls had changed from hate to jealously. Their open disdain had been replaced by an open wanting to be in my place. I raised a hand to hide my smile then squeezed Scotts hand in thanks.

We never talked about my story. I wondered if he'd ask me questions, he had to have hundreds of them. Scott however acted like I hadn't told him a thing. Somehow though, he let me know at the same time that he was there if I needed to talk.

Lunches were my favorite time of day. We'd sit next to each other our shoulders and knees rubbing and laugh at each other's jokes. Mattie and Kevin would stare at us and shake their heads at our weirdness. She'd say stuff like "Gross" and "Get a room" but I knew she was okay with it. Scott would laugh and shrug his shoulders.

One afternoon in the lunch room I caught Gina staring at us. Danny had his back turned to her as he talked to his buddies. For a moment a look of loss and pure hate crossed her face. She didn't want Scott but she didn't want anyone else to have him either. I caught her eye and smiled back the most sickening and triumphant smile one girl has ever given another. You know that whole "I beat you and you will never have it this good look." That look that only another girl could understand. I don't think I have ever felt more pleased with myself.

A couple of weeks after the dance Scott met me after my third period chemistry class.

"Come on let's get out of here, this place is driving me up the wall."

"We can't leave?" I said in shock.

He studied me for a moment and said, "Katie, you've got to skip at least once in High School. It's a rule. Do you want to tell your teenage grandkids that you never skipped in high school? They will think you're the un-cool grandmother. Man that would so suck."

I grabbed his hand and laughed as we raced out of the building. It was a couple of days before I realized we were both over eighteen and could have signed ourselves out any time we wanted.

It was the first beautiful day of spring, a crystal clear blue sky with a giant yellow sun trying its best to warm up the cold earth. The snow had melted and left a hard mud in the parking lot. A cool breeze blew through the trees ruffling bare limbs and sending my hair into a feathery mess.

He took me to the river park and pulled into an empty parking lot. It looked like we were the only ones there. It was too early for moms and strollers. The joggers wouldn't be out until after work. It was only us.

The baseball fields sprouted a fresh green carpet of new grass and off in the distance thousands of yellow daffodils had shot up through the scattered leaves under the trees. It all looked like a Matisse painting.

We slowly walked the path into the trees and along the river. When we were out of sight he pulled me into his arms and kissed me until my knees felt like they were going to buckle. The boy was definitely a champion kisser. He wasn't very demonstrative in public. In private however, he couldn't seem to help himself. Believe me I'm not complaining but it could make a girl worry.

At first I'd thought it might be because he was embarrassed about being seen with me. It was only later that I realized he was being a gentleman. Concerned for my reputation. It made me love him all the more.

My hands instinctively went to his neck and started to slip inside his collar. I needed to feel his skin. Caressing his neck I found a metal chain. It surprised me. He never wore jewelry. He didn't even wear a watch. My mind flashed back to his barn the night Star was born. He'd taken his shirt off, twice. He hadn't been wearing a necklace or chain.

My curiosity got the better of me. I broke the kiss and worked the chain out of his shirt while he was still too confused to understand what I was doing. It was a simple metal link chain. The kind kids used for the house key. He or someone had punched a hole through a penny and hung it on the chain. My curiosity was now up to a hundred percent. I slipped it over his head before he could react. For an outstanding athlete with unbelievable reflexes, he could be slower than a sick snail when we kissed. I smiled to myself when I thought about how I affected him.

I turned the penny in my hand but I couldn't see anything remarkable. "What's this?" I asked.

"Give it back Katie," He said with a frown.

## Certain Rules

Now my curiosity had pegged out at the top. A devilish feeling of power washed through me and I scrunched the chain and penny into my fist and hid it behind my back.

"Take it," I teased.

I knew perfectly well that he could force my arms into any position and easily pry my hand open to remove the coin. I also knew he was no more able to do that than he could hit me or push me down. It wasn't in him.

His eyes turned from happy teasing to a frustrated scowl.

"Come on big boy, I'm not a piece of your grandmothers china, I won't break."

He shook his head, "Katie, you don't understand. I'd never intentionally hurt you, you know that. It's just that, sometimes people get hurt when we're playing around. I broke Justin Blake's arm in fifth grade when we were playing red rover. I knocked out Tim Swenson's front two teeth in ninth grade while playing tag and neither of us were even It. Come on give it back to me." he said holding out his hand.

"No," I said backing up. I had to get him to treat me like a normal person. We had to get rid of those egg shells. "Not until you tell me what it's for or until you catch me," I said then took off running.

I thought I was doing pretty well. I must have gotten fifty feet before he caught up. I turned off the trail and into the trees as he reached for me. Squealing and laughing as I avoided his grasp. Several more times he almost got me. Like I said I thought I was doing great until I realized I was out of breath and he wasn't even breathing hard. He could have caught me any time but was letting me win.

I grew angry and shoved at his chest. "No fair, you've got to try," I said. Of course the big behemoth didn't move and I bounced back three feet. He caught me before I could fall and picked me up to swing me in the air with only one arm.

My feet flew out from beneath me and all the air in my lungs leapt out as I squealed. Instead of putting me down he placed both hands on my ribs and lifted me above his head like a he was pressing a bar bell.

My hair fell forward and covered us both. Our eyes locked and he smiled.

"I can do this all day Katie, Please give me my penny."

I laughed; it was like being on a rollercoaster. What if he dropped me? Deep down I knew I was safe, but there was enough doubt to make it fun.

"No secrets Scott, you know the rules," I said. We hadn't really talked about it. I'd automatically assumed that he knew it was one of my rules. My stomach lurched, if he could keep this a secret, what else could he be keeping from me?

He thought for a moment while I continued to hang there in the air.

"It was my dad's," he said.

I of course felt like a complete idiot. Why else would he carry around a penny on a chain?

"It was in his effects they gave me at the funeral home. The mortician handed me two brown manila envelopes with their stuff in them. He said he could put them in the coffins if we wanted. I remember opening it and sliding the continents onto the table. A watch, a money clip, a wedding band, and that penny. I don't know why he only had one penny in his pockets. I gave the watch to grandfather and the money clip to Mattie. I'll use the wedding band when I get married." His eyes lost focus for a second and I could feel his arms begin to shake. He slowly set me down and I handed him the chain and penny.

"When we came home from the funeral I found a chain and punched a hole into the penny and hung it around my neck. I figured it had to be a lucky penny now. It'd already gone through a major car wreck. No way could anything bad happen to it again." He sighed heavily. "You see, I had to stay safe, Mattie needed me. I also figured I couldn't kill myself if I was wearing it. Believe me those first few months the question was in doubt."

I stood there and listened to him, my heart breaking at the thought of the little boy searching for safety and security. It seemed we all had our own versions of hell.

He held the penny out and let it swing on his chain like a gypsy's mesmerizing crystal. Taking a big sigh he smiled and slipped the chain over my head. "I want you to have it, it'll keep you safe."

"What, no, you can't give it to me. It was your dad's," I said as I scrutinized the treasure. My heart raced and my palms began to sweat. No one had ever given me such a wonderful thing. I could feel myself starting to tear up. I shoved at his chest trying to lighten the mood. "It's not fair, you're bigger and faster than me. I can never win."

He laughed, "What, you want me to be smaller and slower than you?"

"Well, no, I like how big you are, you're like a mountain, safe, secure, and stable. I'd like to have a fighting chance though."

He laughed and gently took my hand. "Come on let's get back on the trail, I want to steal a couple more kisses.

I reached up and kissed him on the cheek and said thank you as I placed his lucky penny next to my heart.

## Chapter Sixteen

<u>Scott</u>

I wiped the sweat from my eyes as I jogged down the dirt road. My weight was starting to creep up. It might have had something to do with the five thousand calories I was putting away daily. That and the fact that I wasn't busting my hump in practices every day. The sun had called me this morning when I woke up. I decided to hit the road and start getting things under control. My muscles loosened up at the beginning of the second mile. That hard empty feeling settled in and made me smile. It had been awhile.

It was a crisp spring Saturday morning and the prettiest, sweetest girl in the world loved me. Life doesn't get much better. At the end of the second mile I turned and headed home. A guy my size is not built for long distance running. I top out at four miles. Anything more than that and I become a quivering mess.

Besides, Katie and I were planning on spending the day together and heading for a movie in Brady later that night. We were arguing about what to see. She'd win of course, but I wasn't going to make it easy for her.

Finishing my chores after the run I made sure Grandfather didn't need anything more before I took off. A quick shower and I jumped out the door before anybody could change their minds.

Mattie followed me out. She folded her arms across her chest and gave me a bitter sweet smirk. "You're never around anymore," she said with a wistful sound of regret.

My heart broke a little and I wondered if I should invite her along then immediately squelched that ludicrous idea. I sighed and walked back to her. "I tell you what, next time you go out with Kevin I'll tag along and keep you company, how about that?"

She swung and hit my shoulder but smiled at my absurdity then frowned. "Kevin's never asked me out." She looked so sad it broke my heart. I knew there was a little manipulation going on. She's my sister, what can I say. The idea of her going out with boys was terrifying. The idea of her sitting home alone sad and miserable was worse.

"Do you want me to talk to him?" I asked.

She squealed and hit me twice. "Don't you dare, I'd dig a hole and crawl into it if you broach the subject with him. Do you understand?"

"Okay, okay," I said rubbing my shoulders. I never should have taught her how to throw a punch. "Maybe if…."

"NO!"

"Alright, okay, I get it. No big brother involvement."

She smiled and hugged me goodbye.

As I started to climb into the truck I turned back. "Hey Mattie, how about I take you down to get your learners permit after school on Monday, your fifteen and a half right?" She squealed and ran to give me a hug before she walked back to the house mumbling something about a test.

Like I said, life was good.

.oOo.

The date with Katie went its normal outstanding self. She wore a pleated red skirt and a tight black sweater that made her look sexier than a New York model sitting on a cool car. Her glasses reflected back my huge smile, she really didn't like contacts. That was fine by me; the whole sexy librarian look was a real turn on.

While we were in line for the movies several guys I didn't know shot her looks of approval. Running their eyes over her body when they thought I wasn't looking. Katie caught it and shivered. I leaned down and whispered. "I want extra points for not pounding their heads into the concrete. Unless you want me too that is?"

She laughed and shook her head. I made it a point of stepping between her and them and giving them a look that let them know how unhappy I was. They got the message and turned to flirt with some other girls in front of them.

After the movie I drove us to the bluff and turned off the engine. We sat there for a moment staring into the night. I counted twelve yellow porch lights twinkling like static fireflies. This place would always be special. Fleeting memories of what we called "Her Story" popped in and out of my mind. Would they always be haunting us I wondered?

Being a red blood young man of course I had thoughts about the two of us taking it up a couple of levels. Like all the way up. Okay, it was all I thought about. Every waking moment and most of my dreams seemed to be filled with thoughts about the two of us making love. Here I was sitting next to the prettiest, sexiest girl in the entire country and I couldn't do anything about it. The wrong word, the wrong move and I'd scare her away, maybe forever. Heaven knows she had more than enough justification to avoid anything that could make her remember the hell she went through. Maybe counseling could help. Maybe I could find somebody who could tell me how to be next to this wonderful, sexy person and not want her so much.

*"Take it slow"* I kept telling myself. *"Don't screw it up."*

.o0o.

Katie

Scott's left arm was wrapped around my shoulders cradling me on his lap. His right hand was on my hip, rubbing small circles that seemed to penetrate to my very core and set it on fire.

I became lost in the touch and feel of his lips on mine. My world narrowed to just his lips. A warm tender feeling suffused through my whole body. His hand drifted to my tummy and rested half way between my chest and belt. My insides tensed up waiting for his hand to move.

His hand slipped inside my shirt and burned my skin where ever it touched. The heat worked its way into my body and brought it alive. I couldn't stay still and shifted on his lap to get a better position.

Scott gasped and broke our kiss with a reluctant sigh.

"Maybe we should take a break for a minute." His voice sounded like a cement mixer full of gravel as he rested his forehead against mine.

"Okay," I answered my lips pursing in a pout. It hurt to think he didn't want to kiss me. That wasn't really the issue but it still hurt. Scooting around on his lap to get more comfortable I stared out of the steamed up windows.

A moan from deep inside his chest bubbled out and his face scrunched up in pain. I started to jump off him. He clamped his strong arms around me and said, "Don't move, Please for the love of god, don't move."

I can occasionally be dumber than a rock. It took me a moment to realize what was going on. A secret thrill washed through me as I thought about the effect I was having on him. It might have made me a bit of a tease but it was such a sweet empowering feminine feeling. It made me giggle and wiggle a bit more than I should have. He groaned again and gently pushed me off his lap. "You have a mean streak Katie Rivers."

The giggles wouldn't stop as I looked at his face. "No I don't, not really. You caught me by surprise. I can't believe that the great Scott James is embarrassed by little ol' me."

"I'm not embarrassed, I'm frustrated."

A serious pall settled over us. His eyes got big and his pupils dilated. Quickly I held his arm to let him know it was all right, he hadn't upset me. "I know you're frustrated, I am too." The silence dragged on for a moment more.

"I'm scared about taking things further. This has been the most wonderful two months of my life and I don't want to do anything to ruin it. I want it to go on forever. I want it to get better every day."

"I'm not pressuring you Katie. I don't want to be that guy. I love you and I'll wait until hell freezes over if I have too. But that doesn't mean I'm not going to obsess about it in my brain. I'm a human male. It's been proven that we think about little else."

I laughed and sent a silent prayer of thanks that some higher power had seen fit to bring this man into my life. It was unbelievable that we were sitting here calmly talking about sex. If somebody had told me that I'd be sitting in a truck with Scott James talking about making love with each other. I would have thought they were three cards shy of a full deck. The fact that we had already shared our deepest darkest pains made all other subjects easier to breach.

The radio started a new song, it was "AT LAST by Eta James, the first song we slow danced too. It was quickly becoming our song. We looked at each other and broke into huge smiles. The tension was gone and we were okay again. I snuggled into the crock of his shoulder and said "I Love You." He draped an arm around my shoulder and said "I love you more," as he kissed the top of my head.

## Chapter Seventeen

Scott

Walking next to Katie always made me feel bigger, stronger, and more powerful. It was a feeling a guy could get used to, almost addicting.

Holding the door open for her she entered her library ahead of me and deposited her backpack behind the counter. I tossed mine up on my regular table. Mrs. Johnson waived hello then ignored us. She had long ago given up any hope of getting work out of Katie when I was around. I think she was happy for us.

We sat and I pulled out a Trigonometry worksheet I needed to finish. Katie watched me for a minute and unconsciously pulled my dad's lucky penny out and started to rub it. She did that whenever she had a quiet moment to herself.

"What are you thinking?" I asked. It was always impossible for me to read her deepest thoughts.

She startled for a moment then smiled. "I was wondering about my father. I wish I knew him so I could introduce you. Is that weird or what?

"No it's not weird. I wish my mom was still here. She'd have loved you to pieces. My dad would have been jealous."

She smiled and a tear gathered at the corner of her eye. "That is the sweetest thing you've ever said." She buried her head in my shoulder and sobbed. It made me feel weak and useless and I wished she'd stop. Obviously she had a problem and I needed to fix it now.

"You know, maybe we could figure out who your dad is. Your mom had to have gotten pregnant when she lived here. You told me you were born six months after she left."

Katie pulled back from my shoulders her eyes sparkling with unshed tears and a brief flash of hope. "How?" she asked, her voice catching with a weak hitch.

"I don't know but there's got to be a way. I've already asked Grandfather, but he doesn't have any idea."

Katie blanched. "Oh my god, Oh my god," she said, her hand going to her mouth in shock. "Your dad dated my Aunt Jenny, you told me what your Grandfather said. That means he knew my mother also. What if….Oh my god!"

"What if what?" I asked, confused and getting a little scared. Something had really upset her.

"What if your father got my mother pregnant? That'd mean…."

I busted out laughing. It was one of those deep down belly laughs.

"Why are you laughing, this is serious. What if we are brother and sister?" The look of fear and terror on her face was priceless.

I laughed again. "There is no way you are my sister. Believe me, I'd know. I have a sister. I wouldn't feel like this if you were my sister."

"You don't know. Those are social morals established by early religions. You don't know how you would feel about someone you didn't already know you were related to," she said, her face had gone stark white.

All of the color had drained away and I worried about her fainting.

"Katie, I'm positive. You are not my sister. My dad would have been about four years older than your mom. He'd have already graduated before she started her freshman year. There is no way he did that, especially not with your Aunt Jenny's kid sister. You didn't know him. He wouldn't have dishonored our family like that. And if he had, he sure as hell would have married your mom. There is no way."

She looked off into the distance and I knew her mind was running a thousand miles a minute thinking of all the possibilities of how things could go wrong. Shaking my head I stood up and walked towards the book shelf in the back.

"Here, let me prove it to you."

"How are you going to prove it? We may never know. Oh my god, what if we have this hanging over our heads for the rest of our lives."

Then another thought exploded in that brain of hers. "Thank god we didn't do too much," she said and her stark white face started to grow pink then red as she thought about how close we had come a few times.

"Katie, settle down, here look at these." I returned from the stacks with four different year books. All of them were different versions of the same thing. Red and white covers with some kind of tiger on the front.

I found the right year and flipped through the pages until I found what I wanted. Setting it down I pointed out the picture and slid it to her.

She looked at me with terror filled eyes then slammed both hands down on the book, covering the picture of my dad. "No, let's not look. Let's pretend we didn't think about this."

"Katie, come on, listen to me, you can trust me. Look at the picture. My dad doesn't look anything like you. Different hair, eyes, everything."

Slowly her hands slid away from the book as she looked at the picture. She studied it for several seconds then let out a huge sigh as her shoulders slumped in relief. "That's not my father," she said with a shaky voice.

I studied her as she ran a finger over the picture of my dad. "He looks like you," She said. "He has your eyes. I wished I could have known him."

My heart lurched at the pain in her voice. I'd do anything to make her happy. She looked up with glistening eyes and a weak smile.

"Come on," I said. "Maybe we can find your father in here."

We started going through the yearbooks. She squealed when she found her Aunt Jenny with long brown hair and a shy smile. When she found her mother's sophomore picture she froze and stared at it for several minutes.

"She looks so young, innocent, with no idea of what life has in store for her."

I glanced over her shoulder at the picture. I saw a bit of a wild girl with wavy blond hair and too much make-up for a girl her age. She looked into the camera with a challenge and glint in her eye. This was a girl with dangerous written all over her. She looked so different than Katie. Her jaw and forehead were the same. But the blue eyes had a hard knowing look that Katie lacked.

.oOo.

### Katie

My stomach was settling down after the scare of thinking Scott might be my brother. The idea had stopped my heart and terrified me so much I thought I was going to be sick right there in my library.

Blessed relief had flowed through me when I saw Scott's dad. I knew immediately he wasn't my father. A little pang of regret had flittered across my thoughts. I was ecstatic but also wanted to know who my dad was. An envious feeling of jealousy towards Scott bubbled up. He may have lost his father, but at least he knew who he was. Knew his history. Grew up knowing where he came from.

I started going through the year books. Why didn't we think of this earlier? The fashions had changed over the years. Their hair used to be bigger and they wore a lot more pastels. Quite a few of the boys had perms. I laughed, the guys today wouldn't be caught dead with a perm. I looked at Scott and shook my head, I couldn't imagine him in a perm. Continuing to go through the pictures I looked for my eyes looking back at me.

Would I know it if I saw it? I wondered. Each picture was different yet the same. High school kids trying to look cool. Full of potential and excitement about the future.

What were their teenage years like? Was it the best time of their life. Had they peaked in high school and everything afterwards been a letdown? Had they hated high school, fighting to make it through years of embarrassment and not belonging? How many of them had felt bullied, how many of them were the bullies.

I continued to flip pages, my fingers running down the pictures. My stomach kept turning over in worry. What would I do if I found it? What if I didn't? Scott stood behind me looking at the pictures, his calming presence giving me the strength to keep going.

A face jumped out at me. A boy in his senior year. It wasn't any one thing but a combination that froze me in place. The boy wore glasses that looked a little too big for his face. He had brown auburn hair with a reddish tint. Green eyes looked back at the camera with a cocky attitude. It was the facial bone structure, the chin and cheek bones. It was a masculine version of my face to the Tee. It felt like I had seen that face before. I looked to the side of the page to put a name to the picture.

Steven Carrs. Danny's dad. My insides hardened into stone as I gasped. No! Scott's enemy. I looked again, cataloging each feature. Studying the picture trying to find some way to deny the evidence in front of me.

Scott saw what I was looking at and started to rub my back. I looked at him with raised eyebrows. Did he see it? He nodded and gave me a weak smile.

I looked back at the picture. Torn between fearing he was my father and hoping like hell that I had finally found him. It was hard to breath, Scott's soothing caress kept me grounded.

"Do you think...?" I asked him.

"It makes sense of something Danny said to me a couple of months ago."

"What, you didn't tell me you talked to Danny."

"I didn't think it was that important. He confronted me in the parking lot. It sounded like he was trying to warn me away from you…"

"Why would he do that?"

"I think he knows you're his sister. Maybe he was afraid I'd see it and tell everyone."

"Is being my brother such a bad thing," I asked as I looked back at the picture. A brother, the thought had never really occurred to me.

"For Danny it would be," Scott said. "His family is one of those that believes appearances are important. His dad owns the John Deere dealership and is a town councilman. He's always cared what people thought about him and his family."

The picture was mesmerizing. Steve Carrs was wearing a beige suit and skinny black tie, it reminded me of a nineties movie about high school kids. "That isn't proof, this picture isn't proof," I said.

Scott was quiet for a moment letting me think, "You know it's him. Look at it. What are you going to do?"

It was unbelievable, this might be my dad. "I want to meet him, I have to know."

Scott nodded his head and put his jacket on. "Okay, no time like the present."

"What? Now?" My heart stopped and my palms began to sweat. This was going way too fast. No way was I ready for any of this, I hadn't prepared myself. What if it turned out to be wrong? What if he didn't want me coming back into his life? A thousand things could go wrong. Why did we ever go down this path? Life had been great, I had Scott. I didn't need anything more. Putting the genie back in the bottle was impossible. I knew who my father was, I had to deal with it.

Scott got my jacket and helped me slip it on. He squeezed my shoulders and kissed my neck. "It's going to be alright Katie, I promise."

He meant it I'm sure, but I also knew that even Scott can't control everything. A daze descended as I let him lead me to his truck. We were going to meet my father. Maybe?

.oOo.

The John Deere dealership was located on prime real estate at the intersection of Main Street and First Avenue. The large parking lot was covered in green and yellow tractors and giant combines. These machines were what make this community work. Without them we would be a dry prairie supporting a bunch of buffalo and Native Americans. With them these people grew enough food to feed half the world.

Scott parked on the street and held the glass door open for me to go in first. The showroom had smaller tractors and riding lawn mowers with pictures of waving fields of grain on the walls. A salesman jumped up then seemed to deflate when he saw a couple of high school kids coming into his place of business. "How can I help you?" he asked.

My mouth chose that moment to forget how to work, I stumbled over the words. Scott, being Scott stepped in and said "We'd like to see Mr. Carrs please."

The Salesman's eyes jumped to his forehead. "Uhm, is there anything I can help you with, Mr. Carrs doesn't usually meet with customers."

"He'll meet with us. Tell him Scott James would like to talk to him." The man's eyes narrowed in thought then he nodded to himself and asked us to have a seat and he'd go check. The waiting room had some chrome and green vinyl chairs begging to be sat in. Scott led me in and got us situated. I pulled out my last handy wipe. I should have gotten more from my locker before we left school. After I'd wiped off my hands I looked for somewhere to throw the wipe and its packet away. Of course there wasn't a trash can in sight. I started to obsess about the trash in my hands, worrying about putting it in my pocket, what if it fell out while I was talking to my dad.

Scott read my expression and chuckled then held out his hand for the papers. I placed them in his palm. He scrunched them into a ball and put them in his pocket. Nothing ever fazed him. I thanked my lucky stars that I'd found somebody to put up with my many idiosyncrasies.

"What if he doesn't like me," I said.

Scott chuckled again, "I've known Steve Carrs my whole life, and he is a lot of things, but stupid isn't one of them. Don't worry, you'll be fine."

## Chapter Eighteen

### Scott

Mr. Carrs' corner office reminded me of a bank president. A big oak desk dominated the center floor space. With two brown leather chairs arranged in front waiting for big spending farmers looking to lay down hundreds of thousands of dollars for some new farm equipment. A credenza behind his chair was covered in pictures of Steve Carrs with important people. A picture in a gold frame held pride of place in the center showing him shaking the governor's hand, both of the politicians posing for the camera.

A silver frame on the corner showed him with one arm around Mrs. Carrs and the other around Danny. I remembered when that picture had been taken. A couple of years ago I had gone with Danny to the lake for the weekend. It turned out to be a meet and greet opportunity for a bunch of state people looking for the next state representative. Mr. Carrs had spent the evening hobnobbing with the politicians. Danny and I had spent it dancing with the girls from the Lake District.

Katie sat and placed her hands in her lap. Her eyes had been drawn to the family picture and I could almost feel her lose her will to go on. I gently touched her knee with mine.

Mr. Carrs cleared his throat. He didn't look happy. Our eyes locked for a moment. "You have some nerve coming here Scott." He said with that town leader voice. The condescending bastard was in for such a surprise.

"Actually sir, we're not here about me. I'd like to introduce Kathrine Rivers. I believe you knew her mother Margaret Rivers in high school. Or at least she was in High School, you would have been in College by then."

The color drained from his face like a thermometer in the arctic. I actually watched it drain. His forehead went white first followed by his cheeks then his neck until he looked like a shut in ghost. His eyes grew three sizes bigger and his jaw dropped open. It was priceless and I had to work hard not to clap my hands in glee.

Katie stiffened and waited.

.oOo.

Katie

My heart wouldn't stop racing and my palms felt like they were pumping out gallons of sweat. I secretly wiped them on my pants. Studying his face didn't help. He was older than I expected. His hair was starting to turn gray at the temple and he had wrinkles at the corners of his eyes. My heart couldn't tell. You'd think a person would know if the man before her was her father or not.

There was no hints in his office. The picture of his family made me scan Danny again looking for any similarity. Maybe, I thought.

"... knew her mother," Scott said.

I drug myself back into the conversation and realized what Scott had just told him. No leading up to it. He'd dropped it like a bomb right there in the middle of his office. I watched the color drop from Mr. Carrs face and my racing heart came to a screeching halt as our eyes

## Certain Rules

locked and I saw recognition. He knew I was his daughter I could see it in his eyes. Maybe.

He gathered himself and pondered for a moment how he should respond. Finally his shoulders slumped and he nodded. "Yes, I knew her. How is your mother?" he asked me. His eyes scanned my face as if he was trying to remember every detail.

"I really don't know. I haven't talked to her for a couple of years."

"I'm sorry," he said, his eyes narrowing in concern. "What can I do for you?" His voice caught for a moment as if he was dreading the answer.

"Are you my father?" There, I'd asked the question. The thousand pound gorilla in the room could no longer be ignored. I held my breath.

He hesitated for a moment then slowly nodded his head. "Yes, I think I am. You look exactly like my mother at your age. I have a picture of her in high school in the sixties and you two could be sisters."

A grandmother? Was she still alive? A thousand questions flew through my mind. I didn't know which one to ask first. Instead we stared at each other across his desk. He didn't seem upset about the whole thing, but he wasn't overjoyed either.

"Did you know about me?" I asked. Unspoken was the issue of why he hadn't ever tried to contact me.

He rubbed the back of his neck. Sweat stains had appeared under his arms. "Not really, your mom told me about her being pregnant but I wasn't positive I was the father. Before I could find out for sure, your mom disappeared. I figured she'd left town to have an abortion or put you up for adoption."

I flinched and felt as if someone had smacked me in the face. He talked about abortion or adoption like he was talking about a tractor going in for repair. Not a human being, not his daughter. He saw my reaction. His eyebrows scrunched together in concern but he didn't say anything else.

The oppressive silence filled the room like a force of nature. Each of us looked at the other, what next, I wondered.

"Danny's birthday is in October isn't? Katie's is in November. Interesting," Scott said.

Mr. Carrs, my father, grew embarrassed, his eyes shifted down for a moment and he started to turn a little pink. He cleared his throat again and then nodded. "I didn't know my girlfriend, Danny's Mom, was pregnant when I was... I uh was with your mom." He hesitated a moment before going on. This was obviously not easy. "I found out about your mom about a week after I found out about Diane." He glanced at the family portrait on the corner of his credenza. "To say I was surprised is an understatement. We'd only been together once and she told me she was on birth control."

"And you were in college by then and she was what a sophomore in high school?" Scott said.

"Hey she was legal. Sixteen was of age back then."

"Does your wife, Danny's mom know."

He sighed and looked away from us for a moment as he was recalling something. "Yeah she knows. When you moved back to town I figured things out and wanted her to be warned. I didn't know you'd wait two years before approaching me."

"You've known for two years and never said anything, never tried to contact me."

"Like I said, I wasn't sure I was your father. I don't mean to be unkind, but your mom had a bit of a reputation. I wasn't sure until you walked in here today. You look too much look like my mother."

The ability to speak had left me. It seemed to be happening a lot lately. The silence descended again. I didn't know what to do next. I hadn't thought this through.

"What now?" He was probably worried about the kind of stink I could cause in town, bringing up old stories. The shame I could heap on his family.

I looked at my father. I took off the rose colored glasses, got rid of the wishes and saw a simple small town businessman who had made a mistake when he was in college.

"I just wanted you to know, that I knew, that you knew I was your daughter. If that makes any sense. The next thing is up to you." Smiling to myself I got up and left the office before I broke down in front of him. Scott jumped up and started to follow me out then stopped and turned back to my dad.

"She's a special girl, you're lucky to have such a daughter, don't screw it up," Scott said to him before he caught me in the hall. I fell into his arms and leaned on him as we made our way out of the building.

He immediately drove us to our spot on the bluff. It was strange looking at the valley during the daylight. The farms were broken into green and brown squares. Some of it freshly turned earth being prepared for the spring planting. Other fields were a fuzzy green from fresh winter wheat coming in. In the far distance a tractor created a small dust storm as it plowed a field. I wonder if they had bought the tractor from my dad.

"What you thinking about?" Scott asked.

I scowled at him from under my brow. "What do you think I'm thinking about?"

"Okay, you're thinking about Mr. Carrs, the questions is. What are you thinking about him?"

"You don't have to call him Mr. Carrs, you can call him my father, or even my dad. Just because he could care less doesn't mean we have to tip toe around the subject. We have enough egg shells around here as it is."

"What did you want him to do? I mean …. In a perfect world what did you hope he would do?"

"I don't know. He's the adult in this situation. I expected him to know what to do next." A life time of fantasies and day dreams down the drain like yesterday's soup. "I guess I wanted him to take me in his arms and hug me and tell me he was sorry. I wanted him to go to the top of his roof and yell to the world that he had a daughter and she was the greatest thing ever. I don't know, I guess I wanted him to give a shit." My voice was rising and I probably sounded like a harpy screeching for its lunch. I didn't care. Scott went to put his arm around me but I slipped away and into the corner of his truck. The last think I wanted was to be comforted. I was enjoying being mad.

Scott wisely folded his arms across his chest and stared out the front window. Yes I was overreacting, I couldn't stop myself.

The silence between us grew until it almost matched the drowning silence in my dad's office. "I'm sorry for snapping at you, this isn't your fault," I said. He continued to stare out the window, his arm muscles bunching and tensing up. His jaw looked like he was grinding his teeth into dust. Great, now I've pissed my boyfriend off. It seemed I was good at making people mad at me.

"What are you thinking?" I asked him as I looked out from under my brow.

He sighed then thought for a moment. "You've got to let me help you when you need it."

"Something's can't be helped."

"I know," Scott said. "That doesn't make it any easier. When I see you hurt or upset, it drives me up the wall. I want to pound what is ever bothering you into oblivion. Of course I'm aware that is not always the best response, but …. I can't change."

The distance between us felt as wide as the English Channel. I scooted over and buried my head on his shoulder. "I know, I'm sorry."

He hugged me and said how he was sorry too. Everything was fine again and I was able to breathe.

After a few minutes he said, "So basically, your mom's in Jail, your dad's an asshole and your brother betrayed me with my girlfriend. Tell me again why we're together."

## Certain Rules

I laughed into his shoulder. "Because you love me, and because I love you more."

"Yeah, buy I love you the most," he said.

## Chapter Nineteen
### Scott

Things were going good between Katie and me. We talked about her father, trying to decide whether we should tell anybody else. Did she want everyone knowing that kind of thing? She decided that she'd tell her Aunt, she didn't want her learning from some busybody in town. Otherwise, she'd keep quiet and see what happened.

Of course that didn't take into account what Danny would do. He chose to act like his regular jerk self and made a serious mistake.

Katie and I were walking in school on our way to first period. I'll admit I wasn't really paying attention; she had a way of capturing my full awareness. We turned a corner when Katie was pulled away from me. Danny had a hold of her upper arm in a death grip. He'd blended in with the crowd because he wasn't surrounded by his usual clique of boot lickers.

"What have you done," He yelled, his face inches from hers. Katie's eyes widened in fear and her face went white with pure terror. I knew she was flashing back to her bad time. My world literally went red, crimson smog covered everything. My vision narrowed, all I could see was his hand with its white knuckles gripping her.

Without thinking I grabbed him under his arms and threw him against the lockers. A loud metallic squeech echoed from his back where he hit the metal. I knew that I'd dented it, or better yet he'd dented it. His feet dangled about six inches off the ground as my fully extended arms held him up against the lockers. I didn't care if I'd crushed his vertebra. I wasn't letting him go until I knew Katie was unharmed.

His eyes had bugged out like a beetles as he took a swing at me. I was able to avoid the punch while keeping him pinned. He didn't really have a choice but had to play dirty, it was the only choice he had as he tried kicking me in the groin. I easily stepped aside. His eyebrows narrowed and his shoulders slumped with frustration. He was well and truly trapped. This was the point where I should have brought my knee into his balls. I could have ended everything right then and there. Everything was set up perfect. He had given me license.

Katie placed a restraining hand on my arm before I could finish him off. "Scott, put him down Scott." She kept saying. "Please don't hurt my brother."

A gasp went up from behind us. That had to be Gina. The look on Danny's face ranks up there with some of my all-time favorites memories. The emotional pain and sense of utter loss of hope. Plus the humiliation of being held against a locker against his will by his arch enemy. All of it in front of half the school body plus his girlfriend. Priceless. I could see in his eyes that he knew he'd never fully hold their respect and undivided admiration. His head dropped and his muscles relaxed into soft compliance.

Katie was looking at me, her eyes begging me to hear her plea. Both hands resting on my arms and gently trying to pull them down, to let him go. Slowly I started to return to this reality and realize what was going on around me. I continued to hold him there while I looked at Katie, checking out her arm and making sure she was unharmed. Her soft smile was all I needed to know.

My arms started to shake as I lowered Danny back down. He was lucky I didn't drop him, Hell he was lucky I didn't throw him across the hall and then drag him outside to finish things.

.oOo.

<u>Katie</u>

My giant was over reacting again and I loved him for it. Having two boys fighting over me was a little disconcerting. This was a long way from staying hidden, my invisibility was gone forever. I pulled Scotts arms away from Danny and stepped between them. Keeping my eyes focused on Scott's, I gently pushed him back before he could do any more damage.

The kids in the hall were standing around in shock, their eyes bulging and their jaws open in disbelief. Gina looked like she'd seen a snake in her bed. I wondered if she'd heard me calling Danny my brother, had the others heard. So much for keeping quiet about it and letting them decide who and when to say anything. I couldn't worry about that now, I had to get Scott away before he got in trouble.

I tried pulling him away but he refused to budge. It was like trying to push a semi-truck up hill. He didn't move an inch. His eyes looked like they were trying to nail Danny to the wall on a permanent basis.

"Three days detention, James," Coach Carlson said from behind us. He stood there with his legs apart and his arms folded across his chest. An extremely pleased smirk, more like a shit eating grin plastered across his face. I swear the man had been waiting for this opportunity all year. If possible he'd have given him more, but teachers were limited to handing out three days of detention without taking it to the discipline board for a heavier sentence.

Scott shrugged his shoulders and glared at Danny. "Don't EVER touch her again, I don't care if you are her brother, that doesn't give you the right. Get me?" The entire crowd gasped this time. Scott smiled, he had landed a devastating blow with only a few words. The smile spread as he shot Coach a look of disgust then turned and walked away, making sure to grab my hand and take me with him.

It took me an hour to track down Mr. Thompson. I'd ditched Scott telling him I'd meet up with him later. I entered the teacher's room between first and second period. Mr. Thompson tapped a stack of papers on his desk and glanced my way when I came in.

"What does a student have to do to get three days of detention?" I asked.

He paused for a moment and cocked his head like he was trying to figure me out. "Hello, nice to see you too Ms. Rivers."

My shoulders relaxed, it wasn't going to do any good to piss off another teacher I told myself. "I need to get three days of detention, what do I have to do?"

He smiled and returned to arranging his previous class's tests. "Well this is as first," he said, now it was his turn to shrug his shoulders. "That depends, but basically, anything that upsets school harmony or generally pisses off a teacher. Why do you need detention may I ask?"

## Certain Rules

Shaking my head in answer I scrambled in my brain to find something that would work. Maybe I should just ask for it. "Would you give me detention, three days? They won't let me into detention hall unless my name is on the list."

Mr. Thompson studied me for a moment. "What did Scott do this time?" he asked with a smile.

"It was totally justified, I swear, Coach Carlson has it out for him." I knew the Mr. Thompson didn't particularly care for Coach Carlson, Every time they were in the same room together you could tell by his body language.

"So you think going to detention with him will help how?"

"He's going there because of me, because of something I did."

"It's not a death sentence, a few days sitting in the cafeteria after school won't hurt him, it'll give him a chance to catch up on some of his homework," he said as he started to put his papers into his briefcase. He shut the case and picked it up by the handle ready to leave.

"Listen you damn idiot, do I need to ruin your next class, just give me the damn detention." Sometimes it was fun to be me. Several of the students who had recently entered winced in shock. Somebody whistled in admiration. Mr. Thompson saw the reaction I'd created then nodded. "Very well, Ms. Rivers, three days of detention. I hope you have a good time together."

I smiled as I reached out and hugged him. The world was normal again, everything would be all right. Scott couldn't get mad at me for my crazy family and all the problems they caused him. No way could he get mad if I was sharing his punishment, right?

.o0o.

"What in the hell did you do?" Scott yelled at me when I told him about going to detention with him. He looked like I'd stabbed him in the back. My insides bunched up like somebody had punched me in the gut. I thought he'd be pleased. Why was he mad?

We were all sitting at the lunch table. I'd planned to share my good news before Mattie could start giving him a hard time for getting in another fight.

He was really mad, this wasn't him being upset or worried. He was pissed off.

"Katie, I don't need you trying to protect me or feeling sorry for me for a minor detention." He stabbed at his Macaroni and cheese and shoveled a forkful into his mouth.

It was a shock, I'd expected him to be pleased. We'd be able to spend that time together. I was letting the school know that I supported him. To have it thrown back in my face like this was unbelievably hurtful. This wasn't a mistake on his part, it was intentional, and he meant every word.

I threw my unopened yogurt and fresh orange back into my brown bag and bumped him hard with my shoulder as I stood up. Giving him my most disgusted look, I turned and stomped off. I didn't care what anybody thought.

To top it off, it occurred to me that now we'd have to spend the next three afternoons together in detention.

.oOo.

Scott

Katie walking away like that made my stomach knot into a tight ball and squeezed my heart like a set of vice grips.

Mattie shook her head at me and said, "I swear Scott, you are making Kevin and frogs everywhere seem smarter every day."

.oOo.

I took us to the bluff after the post school detention. Mattie had rode the bus home earlier. Katie and I hadn't had a chance to talk all day. She seemed to be avoiding me. In detention Mr. Thompson separated us before we could sit down.

Katie sat on the far side of the truck. She hadn't sat in the middle seat and kept shooting me expectant looks like she was waiting for something. I turned the truck off and leaned back with a big sigh.

"I'm sorry, I didn't mean to jump all over you like that," I said. She relaxed then nodded her head as she accepted my apology.

"You hurt me Scott, I was only trying to help," She said.

"I know, I know, I'm sorry," I said with my best contrite voice.

She studied me for a moment then unbuckled her belt and scooted across the seat to sit next to me. My arm slipped around her shoulder and pulled her into a tight hug. My insides relaxed for the first time that day and I felt like all was right with the world again. It always amazed me how this young woman had become the center of my life. If she was unhappy, I was miserable.

Snuggling into my side she asked me if I'd any plans Saturday night.

"No, nothing in particular, whatever you want?" I said then wondered if I was assuming too much thinking she'd automatically want to spend her Saturday evening with me.

"Do you want to come for dinner, about six?" She asked with a hesitant hitch in her voice.

"Sure, sounds great," I said. I could feel her smile next to my side.

"It will just be the two of us, Aunt Jenny's going out of town, some kind of training thing for her work. She won't be home until Sunday afternoon."

Home alone with Katie, my heart skipped and a thousand thoughts jumped through my brain. Only a majority of which involved some less than pure actions on our part. "That sounds great, do you want me to bring anything?"

"No, I'll take care of everything," she said before drifting off into a contemplative silence, probably figuring out what she was going to serve for dinner.

We drove home in a comfortable silence, everything was forgiven and forgotten. Having Katie sitting in the middle seat was so much cooler. That was one of the many good points about Katie, she didn't hold a grudge, it wasn't in her.

Walking her to her porch she grabbed my hand and jumped onto the step turning to face me. Her eyes were alight with secret mischief. What was she up to now?

"I'm looking forward to Saturday night," I said.

She smiled as she looked down at her hands. Seeming to come to a decision she looked up and kissed me briefly. Looking deeply into my eyes she asked me to do her a favor.

"Sure whatever you want," I said.

"Can you make sure to bring some condoms?" She said with a smile before turning and skipping into the house.

## Chapter Twenty
### Scott

The damn bolt wouldn't slide into the hole. I was buried under the combine changing out the starter and couldn't get the damn thing to line up. Cursing, I punched it with the heel of my hand and heard it click into place.

My day had been like that since I woke up before sunrise this morning. It started with me knocking my alarm clock off my bedside table and breaking the face plate. I burnt my toast for breakfast, broke a shoelace putting on my boots and now I'd scuffed up my hands trying to get this damn thing into place.

Everything I touched seemed to fall apart in my hands. But hey, I wasn't nervous or anything. I wasn't obsessing about what Katie had said to me the other night before skipping inside her house. No not me. I only thought about it for the thirty fourth time in the last hour.

The day was dragging and seemed to be taking forever. I swear the sun had got stuck. Finishing with the starter I gathered my tools and wiped my hands on a dirty rag. Mattie came out of the barn as I exited the equipment shed. She smiled and joined me as we walked to the house.

"How's Chrissy and Star?" I asked.

"There fine," she said absently as she looked out over the fields. Something was on her mind. She was as obvious as a hairy mole on a super model.

"How are you doing Sis?" I asked.

Dropping the hand that had been shading her eyes she looked at me as if just now realizing I was standing there. Her eyes clouded but she shook her head. "I'm fine. Everything is great." I didn't believe a word of it but also knew I'd never get it out of her until she was ready.

"You know I'm here if you ever need to talk?" I said. Sounding all big brotherly.

She clapped a hand on my shoulder and laughed. "Yea, right, like you're going to tell me how to get a guy to like me. Do you have suggestion on how I should do my hair, Maybe I should ask Grandfather what dress I should wear? Maybe you and I could discuss my p……., Never mind."

My throat hurt from swallowing so hard. Boy had I stepped into it. Those were the last things I wanted to discuss with my little sister, especially today.

Mattie laughed again, "Don't worry, you're off the hook. Go get ready for your date with Katie. Where are you guys going?"

"She's making me dinner at her house." There was absolutely no reason to tell her that Aunt Jenny was gone for the night.

"ooooooouw. She is getting serious. You do realize how important this is to her, right."

I nodded my head but I think Mattie and I were looking at it differently. "Just so I'm sure I'm on the right track here, why is this more important than a normal date?" I asked. Hey information could be gold in this situation. Especially when it came to dealing with women.

Mattie laughed and put her hands in the back pockets of her jeans and slowly walked towards the door.

Hurrying to catch up I bent over to make sure I heard her answer.

"It's important because she's in charge. Until now you've probably been the one to decide where you go, what you eat, etc. You've been the one paying for things. Now you're going to be judging her, judging where she lives, how she cooks. It's an unconscious try out for being a wife. Preferably your wife."

"A wife!" I sputtered. "It's way too early for that. No way is that what's going on." My voice caught on several of those words, especially the one starting with wife.

"I said it's unconscious. She's not thinking like that. But deep down that's what's going on. She's going to be very nervous so you be nice to her."

"Hey I'm always nice to her," I said, reminding myself to stop by the grocery store and pick up some flowers. Husband and Wife, wow, Okay I'll admit that phantom thoughts about Katie and I growing old together had passed through my mind occasionally. And I was very aware that I couldn't imagine us not together. That meant that eventually we'd either have to marry or break up. My stomach tightened into a sick ball thinking about breaking up someday. We wouldn't be like this for the rest of our lives.

Wow, this was some scary shit. I caught up to Mattie as she entered the house and thanked her for the insight. She smiled and I wished I could do the same for her.

.oOo.

## Katie

Nothing was going right. The day was going to be a total disaster. Ever since Aunt Jenny left this morning things had been going wrong.

I'd spilt a bottle of pine sole in the bathroom and now the house smelt like a hospital. A pimple was threatening to erupt on my forehead. I mean come on, I hadn't had a pimple since I was sixteen, now, today of all days. He was going to think I was a Cyclops. Dinner had bubbled over, twice, I was lucky it hadn't stuck to the bottom of the pot.

To top it off, I couldn't decide what to wear, What if he showed up in jeans and a T-shirt and I was dressed all fancy. Or worse, what if he wore a suit and I was in a T-shirt and Jeans. I'd have died right there on the spot.

Inspiration struck, I'd wait until he had left his house then call Mattie and find out what he was wearing. She'd understand. I picked out two different outfits. Jeans and a T-shirt and a green satin dress I had bought last weekend especially for this night. I also laid out my new under things, black, frilly bra and panties. I would be wearing them which ever outfit I selected.

A quick sweep of the house one last time before I jumped into the shower let me know that was everything really was going to be fine. Please god. I checked off the things I'd done that day.

Hugged Aunt Jenny, I had told her that Scott was coming for dinner and that we'd probably watch TV afterword. Her eyebrow had cocked itself half way up her forehead but she didn't say anything. Instead she smiled and patted my cheek. "Have fun dear, call me if you have any problems. I'll be home early Sunday afternoon. I waived to her as she backed out of the driveway before racing into the house and started cleaning it from top to bottom. That was when the Pine Sol accident happened.

Undressing before getting into the shower I caught a glimpse of myself in the bathroom mirror. Pausing, I examined everything. Flat stomach, perky breasts, I should be okay. My hips looked like they'd grown two inches in the last six months though, maybe Scott would think I was curvy. Everything looked acceptable, not outstanding, but acceptable. The issue though was would Scott find me acceptable. As was normal, any thought of Scott sent my brain flying to thinking about tonight and what was going to happen. My body craved him, wanted to touch and be touched. A physical burning in my very center threatened to overrule everything. Please don't freeze up. Don't ruin this, I kept telling myself.

An hour later the doorbell rang as I was putting on the last bit of mascara. My heart dropped and started racing at the same time. A quick once over showed that the bathroom was ready, no embarrassing feminine products or forgotten panties. Running my hands down my dress I thanked Mattie once again for letting me know he was wearing a dress shirt and tie. That's my boy, I thought. He gets how important this is.

I scanned the living room and my face in the hallway mirror before I opened the front door.

My man and his broad shoulders filled the entire outside world. He smiled and my heart melted. He stepped in and handed me the most beautiful bouquet of red roses. Had a girl ever been so lucky? Their scent filled the room and helped hide the last remaining bit of pine sol. Reaching up I kissed him on the cheek and used my thumb to wipe away a faint trace of lipstick. I wrapped my arm through his and pulled him into the room. It was impossible not to touch him. It was like he had been away for ages. You know you've got it bad when twenty four hours felt like a life time.

"Something smells very very good," he said heading for the kitchen. His stomach rumbled and I laughed.

"You have to wait a few minutes; there are a few things that need to be finished."

He totally ignored me and removed the lid off the sauce.

"Spaghetti?" he asked, his eyes lighting up with anticipation like a little boy on his birthday morning.

"Yes, from scratch, Mrs. Carlucci's officially true Italian recipe. Brought from the old country in her mother's hat box she used to say. Now get out of there and let me finish," I said as I tried to push him away from the stove.

He laughed and sat on the other side of the breakfast bar and folded his arms across his chest. Pretending to pout a little. He looked absurd and I laughed.

A delicious thrill washed its way through me as I felt his eyes traveling up and down my body while I worked over the stove. A girl could get used to this. Red roses, a big sexy man waiting to be fed, and thoughts of what was to come.

Slowly, I moved the wooden spoon through the sauce in long, languorous circles, my mind wondering into forbidden areas. "What are you thinking about?" I asked innocently over my shoulder.

"You know what I'm thinking about. I'm thinking about the last thing you said to me yesterday and what that means."

My face flushed and I'm sure I grew three shades redder than his roses. "Yeah, well, we can talk about that later. Help me get the salad on the table while I finish this up.

.oOo.

Scott James eating my cooking at my dining room table had to be one of the most sensuous things ever invented. The way he slowly savored that first bight, rolling it around in his mouth. His eyes closed for a moment as if he was in prayer then a giant smile broke across his face.

"This is unbelievably wonderful, WOW," he said before scooping up another large bight. I lost his attention for a moment as he concentrated on his spaghetti. "No I mean it, this is good. You have got to give Mattie the recipe."

We ate in silence for a few minutes then he looked up and smiled. "You look great by the way. I should have told you when I came in. I really like that color on you. It matches your eyes." I blushed again and felt all tingly inside.

When he dished himself thirds I knew the dinner was a success. He saw me watching him and shrugged his shoulders and said, "Hey, I'm a growing boy, cut me some slack."

I laughed and pushed my plate away so I could rest my elbows on the table and my chin on my hands while I concentrated on him. Scott's a pretty simple guy I realized. All he needs is good food and as little drama as possible.

A desperate need to know everything about him crashed over me like an ocean wave. "What's it like being so big and tall?" I asked. I don't know where the question came from. It bubbled out.

He froze in mid-bight then continued on while he thought for a moment.

"I can't walk into a room without everyone knowing I'm there. I stick out like a sore thumb." He laughed and shook it off like it was not a big deal, but I bet that's one of the reasons he didn't like being the center of attention.

"Let's see, I uh, ... have to be careful. Sometimes I can be a like a bull in a china shop."

"I find that a little hard to believe, you are so graceful and have such good body control," I said. He blushed a little and continued to take another bight.

"It used to be a lot worse; I must of broken a hundred things when I was fifteen. Every time I turned around I was knocking stuff off the table or walking into walls. It was pretty pathetic." I smiled to encourage him. He shrugged his shoulders again. "Let's see ... In every class picture, I am always located in the back row, far right. Every one of them. The teachers are always on the left back. Um, the kids used to call me Lurch, and Shrek. The girls were the worse; they knew I couldn't beat them up so

## Certain Rules

they were relentless. That stopped when Danny told them to leave me alone. For a girl, upsetting Danny Carrs was unthinkable."

My breath caught for a moment, would bad memories ruin the evening. Scott however shrugged it off like yesterday's rain and smiled back at me and stared into my eyes. My mouth went dry and I grabbed a glass of water.

"So tell me," Scott said, sitting back and folding his arms. "Do you have any idea how sexy you look, not just now, but all the time?" I sputtered and spewed water across the table. "I'm serious," he continued, completely ignoring my less than stellar table manners. "You are drop dead gorgeous. It pisses me off when I see other guys staring at you. I know what's going through their evil little minds and I want to crush them into a fine dust. Sometimes I think you really don't know, do you?"

This conversation was so not happening, not here, not now. I couldn't stop smiling as I began to clear the dishes. Scott jumped up and helped me. "You're ignoring my questions." Scott said.

"That's right," I answered, pulling out Tupperware for the leftovers, thankful I had something to do to keep busy. He laughed and started filling the sink, "I wash, you dry, you know where everything goes, okay? But I'm not wearing an apron; a guy has got to have some standards."

I couldn't help myself, imagining Scott James in an apron made me snort. Not a little, lady like snort, but a full blown out snort. It was half way between a bark and a sneeze, god how embarrassing. "You don't have to help," I said as I tied Aunt Jenny's apron around my waste.

"No, no, it's the least I can do after such an outstanding meal. Besides, this way I can occasionally rub against you and pretend like it was an accident.

I laughed and had to bury my face in his upper arm to stop from completely losing it.

## Chapter Twenty One

### Scott

Washing dishes with Katie was my new favorite thing. As I handed her a plate our hands touched and our eyes locked onto each other. Her pupils dilated and we could see what was coming. I saw the desire in her glance, the way her body moved. The soft pink glow of her skin, everything told me that she was ready.

You could cut the sexual tension with a knife, it was thicker than a London fog. Her subtly soft honeysuckle and jasmine scent washed over me and seeped into my soul. The sweet laughter in her voice sent shivers up and down my spine and made me want to think up funny jokes just to hear it. Every soft curve and pristine piece of skin begged to be caressed. A deep ache settled inside of me and burned to be let out.

As we stood there in silence she shifted and rested her hip against mine. I forgot what I was doing for a moment and just thought about how she felt. Her soft hip encased in silky dress resting against me. My heart raced and my palms began to sweat even in the dishwater.

Slow down Scott I kept telling myself, you'll scare her away.

Before I could stop myself I turned and placed my hands on her hips then lifted her onto the counter top.

Her eyes got as big as saucers and those perfect lips pursed in surprise, making a delectable O shape that had to be kissed. I stepped between her knees and brought my lips to hers.

Her lips were sweeter than candied wine and warmer than a summer evening. I melted into her and lost myself in the wonder that was Katie.

After several minutes we parted and rested foreheads against each other. Slowly she ran her hands up my chest to the knot at my collars. Her nimble fingers pulled the tie apart and slowly slipped it from around my neck while staring deep into my eyes.

"I love you Katie," I said as I leaned forward, pushing the corner of her dress aside so that I might nibble at the apex of her throat and shoulder. She moaned and arched into me as her fingernails gently raked my back. My hand dropped to the outside of her firm silky leg and gently, slowly, slipped under the hem of her dress and made its way up her thigh.

Unbuttoning the top of my shirt she slid her hands inside and began to caress my chest. It was like being touched by an angel, sending shivers throughout my body. Please I prayed. Don't screw this up, don't let her be afraid

"I want you Scott James, I have never wanted anything so much in my life," she said.

"Are you sure Katie, I don't want you to feel pressured but if you stop me now I might very well die right here on the kitchen floor.

She laughed and jumped from the counter. Taking my hand she led me to her bedroom, looking over her shoulder, shooting me a coy smile that drove me to even higher arousal. My mind raced a thousand miles a minute. This was going to happen.

A soft lamp illuminated the room in an erotic gentle glow. Her bed invited us. A simple twin bed that would force us to lay in each other's arms throughout the night. She turned to face me. Reaching out she took my other hand and pulled me into the room.

My body strummed like a guitar string, every part of my being was attuned to this very minute. All I could think about was getting that dress off and my hands roaming over her body. If onl ...

DING DONG! The damn door bell sounded as if a gong from hell. Both Katie and I froze trying to fathom what had happened.

DING DONG! Again the impatient sound reverberated through us, ruining our moment. "Maybe it's Aunt Jenny and she's lost her key. Oh my god, what if...." Katie said. Her hand went to her mouth and fear sparked thru her eyes.

"Calm down Katie. Maybe it's a salesman. Your Aunt would have called if she was coming back early," I said, praying to every god I could think to that whoever it was could be gotten rid of quickly.

I followed Katie as she approached the door. She turned to tell me something when the doorbell rang again. Whoever they were, they were as impatient as hell. I knew the feeling.

Huffing in exasperation, Katie threw the door open.

A pretty women in her mid-thirties with long blond hair, wearing a tight knit beige dress that clung to every curve stood at the door looking hesitant and a little afraid.

Katie reached out and grabbed my hand,

"Mom?" she said.

.o0o.

<u>Katie</u>

My mother stood in the door way like a phantom from my nightmares. Where? How? Questions continually tumbled through my mind. Beyond unexpected surprise, this ranked up there with finding Atlantis while looking for a toothpick. My vision started to narrow and I thought I might faint. Instinctively I grabbed Scott's hand for support. What was she doing here and why now?

"Aren't you going to invite me in honey?" She asked

Every fiber of my being yelled for me to keep her drama away from Scott or he'd run for the hills.

Prison hadn't been kind to her. Fine wrinkly lines spread out from the corners of her eyes. Her lips looks smaller, less fluffy. Her neck no longer had the long tight tone it used to. My mom was no longer the young woman I remembered.

"Who do we have here?" she asked, her eyes slowly traveling up the length of Scott making my hackles rise. I hadn't known I had hackles until I saw the way my mother looked at Scott.

"This is Scott James….. My boyfriend," I said. Mother's eyebrows rose in surprise as Scott stepped forward to shake her hand. Her eyes focused on his exposed chest where I had unbuttoned his shirt then shifted to my mussed hair and smeared lipstick.

"I'm impressed," she said with a weak smile.

"Nice to meet you Ms. Rivers," He said.

Her small dainty hand looked like a tea cup in a mixing bowl as she shook Scott's hand, holding onto it a little longer than necessary. I don't know if she knew what she was doing. You'd think that someone who'd seen the bad side of life as much as she had would be beyond flirting, but I honestly think she used it as a weapon to keep others off balance. What she didn't know was that it was wasted on Scott, he was oblivious.

"So... Where Is Jennifer?" She asked.

"Aunt Jenny's gone for the weekend," I answered before realizing what I was saying. Mother's eyebrow shot so far up that I thought for sure that it would merge with her hairline. She looked again at Scott then back to me before shaking her head.

A panicked expression crossed Scott's face and he cleared his throat. "Listen, I better be going Katie. Thank you for a wonderful evening. The dinner was great. I'll make sure Mattie gets that recipe from you. Okay?" he said with a smile.

That's my Scott, keep everything normal. My emotional rock was abandoning me to my mother. He couldn't get out of there fast enough. I didn't blame him, I blamed my mother. She'd ruined all of my plans, again.

I reached up and kissed him gently caressing his cheek. "Thank you, for everything. Pick me up on Monday for school?"

He nodded as he leaned down and whispered in my ear "I love you Katie, hang in there. And I want a do over. We have unfinished business."

I blushed and nodded then hugged him good bye. Mom watched from the sidelines neither commenting nor showing any kind of curiosity.

"Nice to meet you Ms. Rivers," Scott tossed back to my mom as he put on his red and white letterman jacket before hurrying out the door. My mom looked at him with open admiration. Who could blame her? The man looked powerful and handsome. I'm sure she was wondering what he was doing with me. Heaven knew I wondered the same thing a dozen times a day.

My mother waited until the door was fully closed before asking me "You're on birth control right. Don't want you making the same mistake I did." I cringed inside. That's what I'd always be, "Her Mistake."

I shrugged it off and faced her. "It's no longer your concern Mom, you sort of lost the right to care when they hauled you off to prison. Remember?" She didn't flinch at my sharp words. It would take a lot more than that to get through her stiff armor but her eyes widened in surprise. I wasn't the mousy fifteen old she last saw in the court room.

My mom didn't know what happened to me in Jimmy's apartment. But I think she had her suspicions. She was already in jail by the time I escaped and her pimp was in jail with her. She'd long since hawked everything she owned to pay for drugs. No bondsman would give her bail money. The last time I saw her, the Judge had banged his gavel formalizing her three to five year sentence. She'd thrown me a regretful look as they led her away in cuffs. A look that said, sorry kid, you're on your own.

"God this place gives me the creeps," she said with a shudder, dragging me out of my dark memories. She ran a fingertip along the fireplace mantle. "How do you like plain old Nebraska?" she asked with a sneer.

"I like it fine." There was no need to go into details about the social purgatory Scott and I were in. In reality it wasn't much different from my schools in California.

"I can imagine. With a boyfriend like that."

"Why are you here mom? I thought you had to stay in the state if you got out on parole?" A sudden thought jumped into my mind. "You didn't escape or anything did you?"

Her rich laughter filled the room. It was a laugh I remembered from my early child hood when she'd pretend she was happy.

"No, no, nothing like that. I'm out on parole. I got special permission to come see you. I have to be back in two days."

"Why," It's not like there was a deep abiding love she felt for me. She had barely written while in jail. A birthday note in November and a Christmas letter in December then nothing for another ten months. I had faithfully written to her every week while I was in foster care. Pretending everything was fine. When I didn't get any responses I panicked, first thinking she knew and despised me for what happened. I figured out she just didn't care. My last letter had been a short note to tell her I was moving to Aunt Jenny's.

It had occurred to me that my mother had returned after three years of separation and we hadn't hugged each other. Not for the first time, I wonder if she felt any guilt about what happened.

"Dad says to say hello by the way," I said and was rewarded when her eyes popped and mouth fell open.

Something had finally pierced her and I felt good to get a little back of my own.

"You tracked him down did you? Is he still married to that Diana bitch?" she asked. Her claws came out and for the first time ever I saw a hint of jealousy in my mother.

"Yes, they are still married, and in fact, their son Danny was Scott's best friend for years. Funny how life works out sometimes." The feeling of pure glee at twisting the knife a little did not make me upset. That might have worried me at another time, but not now, not with her.

She stared off into space for a moment, probably wondering what might have been. She gathered herself and took a deep breath before squaring her shoulders. "It seems California's jails are overcrowded," she said. "They're letting people out left and right."

My stomach dropped as I waited for her next words. Where was Scott, I needed Scott.

"Jimmy got out too," She said as she stared at me watching for my reaction. "I thought you might want to know."

Four words, four little words and my world ceased to exist as everything went black.

## Chapter Twenty Two
<u>Scott</u>

I should have known, should have seen it coming. Maybe I could have changed things. Looking back the signs were all there. Hey I never claimed to understand girls. On Monday morning she had Mattie scoot over instead of waiting for her to get out and let Katie into the middle. I chalked it up to her being in a rush.

The next indication was in first period when she didn't say a word to me all class. Not even a note slipped under the desk. She sat their bighting the corner of her lip and staring off into space. Her books were lined up perfectly with the corner of her desk. She ran her hand along the edge checking the alignment three times. When she pulled out the third handy wipe and opened the package in the open I finally realized she wasn't doing well. I reached over to caress her shoulder and let her know I was there. She cringed and drew away from me like a skittish colt. When the bell rang she was out the door with a quick wave.

Lunch was a boring, lonely hell. Mattie told me that Katie had stopped her in the hall and let her know that she wouldn't be joining us, that she had something to take care of. I cross examined Mattie in detail. Unfortunately she couldn't provide any enlightenment, her confusion matched mine.

Catching up to her during sixth period in the library, I came to a screeching halt. Her hair once again hung across her eyes and she wore a bulky sweater. Spring had arrived weeks ago, the library windows were wide open for Christ sake. From what I could see her eyes were red and puffy, she'd been crying. My heart broke as I walked up to her.

"Are you all right Katie? How'd it go with your mom?" I asked.

Her head leaned forward with her chin on her chest as she focused down at her hands with a frozen stare.

"We can't see each other anymore," she said with a cold, emotionless voice.

My heart stopped then broke into a thousand pieces like a shattered water glass. No warning, no "it's not you, it's me" statement, not even, "We can still be friends", Nothing, simply an exclamation that ruined everything in my world.

I'd been hurt before. I'd dislocated a shoulder in tenth grade. My face had a healthy chunk carved out by a snapped piece of barbed wire. My parents dying in a car wreck. Hell, even catching Danny and Gina had hurt. There are all kinds of different hurts. Nothing like this though. My very soul had been gouged out and left hanging to dry in the wind.

"What... What do you mean?" I asked, my voice cracking for the first time in three years. Maybe I had misheard her.

She shook her head and repeated it. "We can't see each other again,"

"For a while, or forever?" I choked out, dreading the answer.

She hesitated then sighed and her shoulders slumped. "Forever," she said. Bursting into tears before she turned and ran back to Mrs. Johnson's office and away from me.

There comes a time in every guy's life when he is faced with a truly terrifying situation. We always wonder how we'll perform. How will we react when a true crisis arrives? I wish to report that I failed miserably. I didn't chase her into the office, didn't run after her and take her in my arms and change her mind. No not big bad Scott. I stood there in shock, my mouth open and eyes bugging out like a fish on the beach.

I'd lost the ability to calmly think. Everything was blank. The anger started to take over. I could feel it building from the bottom of my shoes and rushing to fill every muscle. I wanted to pound and destroy everything around me.

Yelling "Aaaargh" at the top of my lungs I swung my fist and swept her perfectly aligned books off the counter and onto the floor. Feeling absolutely no better, I stormed out of the library before I could do more damage.

Mattie pestered me all the way home about Katie, where she was, what had happened, what I had done to ruin things. Finally I told her to shut up or she could walk home. I didn't even feel bad about snapping at Mattie. I didn't' know if I'd ever feel anything again.

.o0o.

Katie

The deep dark shame filled every part of my body. Only the pain could fight against it. Scott hurt and I had been the one to cause it. Everything about what I had done to him was wrong. I will never forget his face when I told him. Scott didn't like letting people see inside his feelings. His armor was every bit as strong as my mom's.

All day I had hid from the truth and delayed the inevitable. Putting it off because I couldn't face the truth. Scott and I couldn't be together. We'd never consummate our love. For the rest of my life I'd miss what might have been. I know that it will eat at my soul until I shrivel up and die.

First period was hell the next morning. His huge physical presence inches away. His soft smoky aftershave sent a shiver down my spine. Warmth and that feeling of home poured off of him and into my core. We sat next to each other, neither speaking. Fighting hard to make sure our glances did not cross. Like Ghostbuster streams, if our glances crossed, the universe would cease to exist.

This time, he was the first one out the door. His broad back briefly filled the exit before he disappeared. A sense of loss burned through me. The rest of the day was a blue haze as I walked through the school in a funk.

The library became my safe haven. Every bump or scrape had my eyes shooting to the front door. My heart skipping a beat until I could confirm it wasn't Scott walking in.

A part of me wanted him to change my mind. Or at least try. I was a little hurt that he had given up on me so easily. I know I wasn't being totally fair. He'd let me walk away. Nothing could have changed my mind. I'd not risk it. It would have been nice if he had tried though.

The walk home that day was a surreal experience. The azure blue sky and gentle breeze were screaming spring. A time for love and regeneration. Somebody honked as me as they tore out of the school parking lot. I looked up and was surprised to see my brother's girlfriend give me the finger and turned and laugh with her boyfriend. Danny didn't look too pleased, He didn't try to stop her though.

Great, they hated me when I supported him, now they laughed at me when I cut his heart out. You'd think they'd have something better to do with their lives.

My mind drifted as I unconsciously put one foot in front of the other. My heart kept screaming at me that I had made a mistake. My mind however knew it had to be done.

I was half way home when my shoulders began to itch and a sense of dread settled over me. Somebody was watching me. Was Scott hiding somewhere and following me somehow. I almost jumped with joy. He did care, please help me change my mind I prayed. Maybe he knew of a solution.

The itchy feeling didn't last, maybe I'd imagined the whole thing. I finished the walk home and immediately hit my room. Crawling into bed I tried to push my world away.

.oOo.

Scott

Five days of pain and humiliation. Stomachs weren't mean to go through this much turmoil. Every time I saw her my heart stopped and fists clenched. Losing her had killed me. Not knowing why sent me to hell.

I sat in my bed room lost in thought kicking myself for not taking a thousand pictures of her. Capturing every moment together should have been one of my main goals.

No pictures, no emails. Not even a voice mail message. You'd think that in this day and world I'd have tons of things. The internet was useless. She didn't have Face book or a twitter account. Nobody I knew had tagged her in any picture anywhere. Even last year's year book didn't help. It seems she'd been absent that day. Probably on purpose. Ever invisible.

I picked the sewing needle off my desk. I don't know where I got it from. Didn't really know why I was holding it. My mind sort of turned off as I started to trace the letter K into the back of my hand. A fine red line appeared on the area between my thumb and my index knuckle. If I'd been all there I'd have thought about Harry Potter and the evil words that had appeared on the back of his hand. This was a simple K. About an inch long. My fingers continued to trace the shape, first pulling the needle down the long stroke then tracing the other two parts.

Repeating my movement. I didn't know why I was doing it but I couldn't stop. The first bit of blood didn't shock me, the purple red color beaded into a drop and sat there as if it belonged.

I scraped with the needle, more blood slowly began to ooze from the wound. Stopping for a moment I wiped the hand across my jeans and then started carving again. There is absolutely no telling how long I'd have sat there. I might very well have carved on my hand until my thumb fell off.

Mattie saved me. She knocked on my door to let me know dinner was ready. A simple everyday occurrence. I jumped back into reality. The red K was already starting to scab over.

I was positive that my hand would heal long before my heart.

## Chapter Twenty Three
### Katie

Nothing in this world was right without Scott in it. I'd thrown away my emotional rock. My grounding path to the earth. Nothing could ever replace it. Twelve days. You'd think that things would ease up after eight days. It didn't seem to be working that way.

Aunt Jenny had tried to pull me out of this depression. I'd ignored her and continued to wallow in my pain. My appetite had disappeared, everything tasted bland and unfulfilling. My bedroom walls were crowding me, making me feel as if I was laid out in a coffin.

Unable to stand it anymore I jumped up and headed for outside. "I'm going for a walk," I yelled towards Aunt Jenny.

Warm, muggy air had built up threatening gray clouds in the distance. Tornado weather the locals called it. Ignoring the warning signs, I set off down our street in the general direction of "I don't care," and "to hell with it." With no idea where I walked or why I continued to get away from the house. It must have been an hour or more later when I finally tried to figure out where I'd ended up.

The neighborhood looked like an older development section. Most of the houses were single story ranches with low chain link fences around the front yards. Huge oak trees picketed throughout the area letting you know how long the houses had to have been there. The wide street had cars and pickups parked along the sidewalks and occasionally up into a yard.

Something bothered me, that itchy pain between my shoulder blades had returned and for the first time I realized I was in a part of town I didn't know. I wondered if I'd be able to hear the Tornado alarm way out here. I wondered what I'd do if I did. The people around here were strangers.

I turned and started for home, walking faster now that I had a destination in mind. The itchy feeling didn't go away and was becoming a concern. I twisted and turned trying to find out if somebody was following me. Every girl knows that awful feeling of being in a strange place, alone, and thinking you were being followed. It squeezes your heart and puts your head on a swivel. At the same time, she desperately does not want to appear frightened or worried. Not advertise her weakness or worse, look like a fool.

A deep rumble washed over me from behind. My heart skipped a beat and my palms began to sweat. Scott, I'd wanted to see a black and white pick-up truck. Instead, a baby blue Cadillac rumbled far down the street and slowly approached. I'd seen the same car a couple of days earlier at Aunt Jenny's store. It stood out like a debutant at a rodeo. I stopped and stared as it got closer. The thing was the size of a boat as is glided towards me. At the last moment it made a right turn at the intersection I'd crossed. I breathed a sigh of relief and headed home.

Two blocks later I heard the rumble again as it stroked the itchy spot between my shoulder blades. I glanced over my shoulder and froze. The rumble belonged to a black and white truck. I breathed a sigh of relief only to tense up when I realized who it was and the fact that he was slowing down to stop next to me.

Scott's white knuckles gripped his steering wheel. His right hand was wrapped in a white bandage. I gasped when I thought he'd been hurt. My hands ached to rub away the pain. Leaning over he opened the passenger door and said, "Get in Katie; it's getting ready to pour."

My heart refused to beat, my feet refused to move, and my stomach refused to stop churning. This was a turning point in my life; I knew it deep down in my core. If I got into that truck with Scott I might lose my will. His handsome, adorable face called to me. I wanted those giant arms wrapped around me holding me, keeping me safe. I missed everything about him, his laugh, his curiosity, and his strength.

Without conscious thought I stepped forward and climbed in, making sure to stay as far away as possible. I didn't want him thinking that things had changed.

"We need to talk," he said while he put the vehicle into gear and started up the street. "We've got to end this thing in a way that makes some kind of sense."

My heart broke again when I saw the painful expression flash across his eyes. He looked so lost, the confusion must be killing him. I couldn't do this anymore; he had to know why so he could move on. Maybe, if he moved on, I could also. Deep down I knew it'd never happen, but I could hope. Scott always gave me hope.

"Okay Scott, let's go somewhere we can talk and I'll tell you what happened and why we can't be together."

His shoulders slumped as he fought to control his breathing. "Thanks," he said then thought for a moment. "I don't want to go to the bluffs, not in this weather, we'd be way too exposed," he said before making a U turn right there. "I know where," he said and was quiet until we pulled into Jack's convenient store and into the very parking spot where I'd told him all about my mother going to jail for prostitution.

For a moment a prickly silence fell over us.

"I've got to know Katie, it's eating me up inside. What happened?" He asked while continuing to stare out his front window, both hands gripping the steering wheel so tightly I was worried he'd break it in two. His eyes glistened and his breaths were coming in rapid short bursts as if he'd run a race.

My god he hurt. I could feel the pain rippling off him. What had I done? Hanging my head in defeat I tuned in my seat and said. "It's not you Scott, it was never about you."

He snorted, "Okay then, what, why do this. Everything was perfect the other night. Did you feel like I pressured you? Too much, too fast? What?"

My chin dropped to my chest and my hair fell into my eyes. I desperately wanted to go somewhere else and hide, preferably forever. "My mother came back the other night."

He silently sat there waiting for the rest. "Yeah, so? I was there remember? In fact, we were minutes away from making unforgettable love when she interrupted us. Believe me, I know she showed up. What's that got to do with us?"

I shook my head as a big juicy tear spilled over and started to run down my cheek. He immediately reached for his back pocket and pulled out a handkerchief and handed it to me. I looked down at that Cobalt blue embroidered S and burst into a full blown crying fit.

Through muffled sobs I said, "She let me know that Jimmy had been let out also. It seems that the jails are too full in California."

Again he was silent; I glanced at him through watery eyes and from beneath my bangs. His furrowed brow and confused eyes let me know that he didn't get it. Sighing in exasperation I said, "Don't you see, He's going to come after me. I know he is."

Scott jumped as if I had punched him. "Katie, I'll protect you, do you really think I'd let anything happen to you. Do you think so little of me that you'd think that?" his voice rose in surprise and I thought it would crack. "I'd die before I'd let anything happen to you, you have to know that."

"No, No, it's not like that," I said as I blew my nose into his handkerchief. I'd have to wash it again before I gave it back. *Maybe a dinner ....* No Katie, don't get your hopes up I told myself.

"If his being out of jail is what's bothering you, I can fix that," he said with a smile. "I'll kill him and your problems are solved. See that was easy."

"Scott, be serious."

"Believe me, I'm serious. There is nothing I want to do more than end that miserable skunk's life forever, preferably in a painfully slow way.

"You don't get it."

"No I don't get it, tell me," he said.

"If he ever found out about you and how I feel about you he could use that. He could make me do it all again." My face fell into my hands and my shoulders shook with the sobs.

Scott didn't move from his seat. Instead he reached and slowly rubbed my back. I think he expected me to flinch away. "I don't know if you've noticed Katie, I'm not exactly like other guys. He wouldn't have much of an easy time beating me."

"It doesn't matter, all he'd have to do would be to threaten me with hurting you. You don't know him. This isn't some high school kid. He's a bad man and I know he's coming after me." I looked into his eyes. "It would be worse than dying if he did something to you. I can't, won't let that happen."

"So you're willing to ruin my life, ruin us! To protect me from some imaginary boogey man."

"He's not imaginary, He's real. You weren't there. You didn't go through it. I won't do it again," I whimpered through sobs.

"Jesus Katie, I'm sorry. I know he's real, what happened to you should never be allowed to happen to anyone. I'd do anything to make it as if it never happened but I can't. What I can do is make sure it doesn't destroy the rest of your life."

"Exactly," I said. "That's why we have to be apart. Don't you see, it's the only way?"

He hung his head and shook it from side to side. "What am I going to do with you," he mumbled to himself.

.oOo.

<u>Scott</u>

Katie wiped her eyes with my handkerchief. What a mess. Pure terror filled her eyes. Why couldn't she see? It made my insides hurt to think that she didn't trust me. I know she'd been messed up by the attack, the fact that she functioned and could make it through life made me admire her every day. That didn't mean she could give up on us like this.

The handkerchief looked like it was sopping wet as she turned it around in her hands trying to find a dry spot. Giving up she blew her nose again then wiped her eyes on her shoulder.

"Hold on a second, I'll be right back," I said. "Promise me you'll stay right here."

Katie looked up with red watery eyes, her eyebrows raised in question then nodded her acceptance.

Opening my door I made sure to remove the keys. It wasn't likely she'd take off on me but I wasn't taking any chances.

The sky hadn't changed much, the dark clouds hugged the horizon and the muggy air made it feel like you were walking through a swimming pool. It surprised me to realize we'd only been here for minutes. It felt like hours.

"Tissues?" I asked the clerk. I grabbed a couple of cokes and took them and the tissues to the counter. A motion outside caught my eye. A baby blue Cadillac the size of a small house had pulled to stop in front of my truck. What the …. The guy had the whole figgin parking lot… A bald guy with enough tattoos to cover a naked sheep stepped out of the beast. Most definitely not a Nebraska farmer I thought. My stomach dropped when I realized who it might be.

## Chapter Twenty Four
### Scott

I stood there with my wallet in my hand and my mouth open. This couldn't be happening. The guy looked to be in his early thirties and appeared to be pretty well built. A thick neck, wide shoulders and big arms. Not an easy customer I thought as I left my stuff on the counter and headed out the door.

"Hey," I yelled. He didn't look back. Instead he walked to the passenger side door and yanked it open, reaching in for Katie. My world instantly turned red, all I could see was this guy, all I could think about was that this was the man who had hurt Katie.

Katie screamed and I could see her kicking at him as she tried to scoot away. A soul crushing fear swept through me as I sprinted across the parking lot. The guy, Jimmy for sure, heard me coming and stepped away to face me. His beady eyes narrowed. Katie was right, they did look like lizard eyes. As I ran towards him I lowered my head for the most important tackle of my life. Jimmy didn't react like he was supposed to. Instead of bracing himself, he stepped into my charge and threw a punch that landed against the side of my head like a sledge hammer hitting an anvil. An inch forward and it would have shattered my cheek bone into fifty one pieces.

The punch staggered me. Stopping me in my tracks. I threw my arm out to catch the hood of my truck and stop myself from falling to the ground. Oh my god this was for real. I tried to clear away the stars and stop the ringing by shacking my head back and forth.

Jimmy had turned back towards Katie when he caught the fact that I hadn't gone down. A brief worried look crossed his slummy little face. He'd thrown his best punch, caught me square, and I hadn't gone down. I could tell he was surprised as he forgot about Katie and focused on me.

Like a magician he produced a knife and swept it towards me with a back hand swipe. I sucked in my stomach in and introduced it to my back bone while I jumped back. I felt the knife catch my shirt and heard a faint swish as it parted the cloth.

A warm wet feeling sprang out on my stomach and I realized the knife had cut me. I didn't have any idea how bad it might be. At least my intestines weren't hanging out, at least not yet. For the first time in my life a feeling of uncontrolled terror washed through me. I realized if I lost, this man would take Katie, I'd be dead, but he'd have Katie.

The man was fast. He followed the knife swipe with a left jab towards my right eye. I stepped inside the punch and blocked it to the side while throwing a punch of my own to his solar plexus. He grunted as my fist landed.

This fight wasn't like the movies where we stood back and swung at each other with fake punching sound effects. This wasn't some high school boyhood tussle. This was a prison brawl to the death. Primeval, live or die, kill or be killed.

It would be over fast, I had size and strength. He had speed and the knife.

Jimmy stepped back for a moment. He knew what this had become. A small smile tweaked his lips. This was not the first time he'd been in this situation and he probably felt the odds were in his favor. What he didn't know was that I was willing to die to make sure he didn't get to her. Just as long as I got to take him with me.

My fingers clenched and unclenched into fists as I imagined my fingers around his throat. I stepped in again, bent low, as we slowly circled. He lunged and I caught his knife arm with inches to spare. The man continued to push, trying to drive it into my chest. Gripping his wrist with both hands now I shifted and pulled with every ounce of strength I ever had. His eyes popped open to the size of billiard balls as he realized what I was doing. Using his momentum I pulled his wrist into the truck and watched the twinkle of shiny metal as the knife flew into the air and skidded across the parking lot.

Now we were more even.

He turned and charged before I could recover. His head caught me in the chest. He quickly lifted it to catch me under the chin while he slipped a heel behind me to trip me to the ground. The asphalt dug into my shoulders as I slid across the ground.

He had me, I could see it in his eyes. A few kicks to the head and I'd be done. He stepped towards with a shit eating grin. My stomach lurched as I tried to scramble up. I knew deep down that I wasn't going to be quick enough. Before he could get any closer a screaming angel-demon flew from the truck and jumped onto his back. Katie screeched as she tried to claw his face off. Her fingernails dug into the man's face. He yelled and twisted to throw her to the ground.

Seeing my opportunity I launched myself at him. My shoulders caught him in the bread basket and my arms wrapped up like I had been taught. Eight years of football said that I should push through him and take him to the ground. The evil anger in me said to pile drive his head into the dirt.

My fingers locked behind his back and I squeezed him in a bear hug while I lifted him. Turning, I threw him to the ground. Following him down I made sure my knee landed on his stomach.

He let out a silent scream as I brought all my weight down on him emptying his lungs of any air. I didn't give him time to recover but started to pound his face with my fists.

My red world had turned full crimson by this point. I lost all awareness. I forgot about Katie, forgot about my burning gut where his knife had cut me. My hands were like diesel pistons pounding into his head. Every bit of hate and anger poured through my arms.

Slowly the world began to come back into focus. A police siren pierced my hearing. Katie yelled at me to stop as she pulled at my shoulder.

.oOo.

*Katie*

My heart continued to beat. I don't know how, but it did. Scott was hurt, I know he was, I'd seen the knife cut across his stomach.

For the first time since Jimmy got out of his car, I thought I might survive this. Scott had been amazing. Like a Mother grizzly protecting her cubs. He'd torn into Jimmy without hesitating. Nothing had scared him. He'd disarmed him and beat him to a pulp.

I grabbed his shoulder and yelled, "Stop, please stop." He was covered in blood. So much blood I thought I might be sick right there next to him. Wouldn't that top everything off? He risks his life and saves me. I throw up.

Scott straddled the man on the ground and finally stopped punching. His fists looked like raw hamburger. His eyes had a thousand yard stare as if he wasn't totally aware of his surroundings. My heart went out to him as he shook his head and tried to bring himself back to this reality.

Eventually he focused on me, seeing me for the first time. His shoulders slumped and he let out a huge sigh. "Are you okay," he asked.

My god, the man has been stabbed, cut, scraped, his eye was swelling shut and his fists looked like they had been put through a meat grinder and he asks if I'm okay. I was made mute. I smiled and nodded.

He smiled back and said, "In that case, does this mean we can get back together now?"

"Yes, god yes," I said as I hugged him around the neck. Oh god thank you for giving me this man I thought as a police car slammed into the parking lot lights flashing and siren blaring.

I was going to have a chance at a normal life. No. We were going to have a chance.

## Epilogue

Katie

I loved watching my boyfriend at football practice. I hated the violence, but loved the fact that he got to do what he loved. I sat in the Nebraska University bleachers and finished my English 101 paper while Scott pushed and pounded for the offensive line. Nebraska had a walk on program for non-scholarship athletes and Scott had wowed the coaches enough to make the team. He'd told me last night in bed that they were saying that he had a good chance to start for the team next year.

Scott and I were living together in a small apartment off campus. My dad was paying for it. He hated the idea of Scott living there, but it was a little late for him to get all paternal on me.

My father had found me at the hospital while they were working on Scott. I think Aunt Jenny had called him. He walked up to me and gave me a hug and I let him. We'd never be a real family, but he'd be the grandfather to my children someday. I smiled thinking about having children with Scott.

A horn sounded and I looked up. Practice was over. I scanned the group of men until I located number Seventy Six. My heart fluttered as he turned and found me in the stands. Smiling he jogged toward me. He looked so cute in those tight white football pants. I wanted to squeeze every part of him.

He read my mind as he ran to the railing and leaned in for his kiss. It had become a tradition before he hit the showers. No matter how hard the practice had been he'd always run over.

"I love you Katherine Rivers," he said with a huge smile.

"I love you more," I answered as I leaned down to share a soul searing kiss.

"Maybe, but I love you the most," he said.

## The End

## Acknowledgments

As always, I wish to thank my lovely wife, Shelley Snodgrass. Her support and encouragement were awe inspiring. I want to thank all of my family and friends for being there when I needed them. Thank you.

A special thanks to the Panera Writers Group. Anya Munroe, Eryn Carpenter, Kristi Rose, and John Pelkey. These fine people were instrumental in helping me iron out the fine points and get over the hump. Thank you so much guys.

Finally, this book is dedicated to two outstanding young women, Caitlin Snodgrass and Andrea Reiher. Both of them, strong, beautiful, intelligent, and sweet. No man has ever had two better daughters. This one is for you.

*G.L. Snodgrass*